The Boy Allies With The Terror Of The Seas

Clair W. Hayes

THE BOY ALLIES WITH THE TERROR OF THE SEAS.

CHAPTER I.

UNDER THE SEA.

"One!"

The speaker was Jack Templeton, an English youth and first officer of the British submarine D-16, Lord Hastings, commander.

Frank Chadwick, an American lad about the same age as Jack, the second officer of the under-sea fighter, laid his hand upon his friend's arm.

"Let me take a look," he said.

Jack relinquished to his chum his place at the periscope, and the latter peered into the instrument long and earnestly.

Into the periscope—which protruded slightly above the surface of the water while the submarine was still submerged—came the vision of a sinking warship, and the sight, enlarged by powerful binoculars, was apparent to Frank's eyes.

"She's done for, all right," he said quietly, turning away at length. "Pretty good shooting, I should say."

"One torpedo only," replied Jack briefly.

"You may give the signal to rise, Mr. Templeton," said a third voice, and Lord Hastings, commander of the submarine, stood before them.

Jack turned away in response to this command.

Another moment and the pumps were at work, forcing the water from the tanks. Gradually the submarine began to rise, and at last rode quietly upon the surface of the North Sea.

Followed by Jack and Frank, Lord Hastings led the way up through the little conning tower, opened now that the submarine was above water, and from there to the bridge, only a few feet above the surface of the sea. Here all turned their eyes toward the east, where, less than half a mile away, a German ship of war was slowly sinking by the head.

"A good shot, Mr. Templeton," said Lord Hastings, turning to Jack.

"Pretty fair, sir," was the latter's modest reply, for he had launched the torpedo with his own hand.

Aboard the sinking German vessel all was confusion. Men rushed hither and thither in wild excitement. Officers shouted hoarse commands. Men scrambled wildly about and jumped madly for the life boats as they were launched. So great was the panic that two of the small boats were overturned and the men thrown into the sea.

"They'll be drowned!" exclaimed Frank. He turned to Lord Hastings. "Cannot we rescue them, sir?"

"It is impossible," was the quiet response. "We have no room for them. We are carrying a full crew, as you know, and have no room for another man."

"But it is terrible to let them drown," protested Frank.

"True," replied his commander, "and yet think how some of our merchant vessels have been sent to the bottom without warning and their crews to a watery grave, noncombatants though they were. It is retribution; no less."

Frank was silent, but he stood watching the struggling German sailors with an anxious eye.

Now the officers aboard the sinking vessel had succeeded in gaining some semblance of order from the confusion that had reigned a few moments before, and the enemy was going about the work of launching the boats more coolly and successfully.

At last all the boats and the crew had left the ship — all but one man, who still stood calmly upon the bridge. This was the commander, who, rather than leave his ship, was preparing to go down with her. In vain did his officers from the boats call upon him to jump. To all their calls he turned a deaf ear, and stood calmly at his post, with folded arms.

Now the sinking vessel began to settle more swiftly. Suddenly she seemed to leap clear of the water, there came a thundering roar, and then, seeming to despair of her efforts to keep afloat, she dived, in another moment she disappeared and the waters of the North Sea closed with an angry swirl over the mighty German warship and her gallant commander.

"Well, she's gone," said Jack quietly.

"Then we may as well go also," declared Lord Hastings. "Shape your course due west, Mr. Templeton."

"Very good, sir," replied Jack, saluting, and he disappeared below.

Lord Hastings and Frank continued to peer at the flotilla of German small boats, which, at a command from the officer in charge, had shipped their oars and were pulling toward the east with lusty strokes.

"I hope they make land safely, or are picked up," said Frank.

"So do I," replied his commander. "Come, we shall go below."

The D-16 again on her way, Frank betook himself to his own quarters, which he and Jack shared together. Here he was surprised to see the latter cutting a notch on the side of the highly polished small table in the center of the cabin.

"What are you doing there?" he asked in surprise. "What are you cutting up that table for?"

"Well," said Jack, "in reading some of your American literature, I learned that every time one of your wild westerners killed a man he cut a notch on his gun. I'm following along the same lines, only I intend to cut a notch on this table every time we sink one of the enemy."

"Quite an idea, that," said Frank. "But when you say you read that stuff in American literature, you are wrong. I won't deny that you have read it, but I'd call it American fiction, not literature."

"Never mind," said Jack, "it'll answer my purpose, whatever you call it."

"Guess I'll turn in for a couple of hours," said Frank. "I'm feeling rather tired."

"Help yourself," replied his friend. "I want a few words with Lord Hastings."

He left the cabin, while Frank, kicking off his shoes and removing his coat, threw himself down on his bed, and in a few moments was fast asleep. As he is taking much needed repose, we will take the time to introduce these two lads more fully.

Jack Templeton, the son of an Englishman, had spent the better part of his life in a little village on the north coast of Africa. His father, who owned a small store, had been his only instructor, but in spite of this the lad had been given a first-class education. He was well read in literature and history, could pass muster on almost any other subject and was well posted on current events.

Jack's father had been taken suddenly ill and after a protracted sickness died. Jack took charge of the store. One day a ship put into the harbor and several sailors landed, went to the store and procured provisions. In Jack's absence, they departed without making payment.

Jack returned a little while later, and when he learned what had occurred, he put off in a small boat after the ship, which he reached before she could get under way.

Now Jack, though young in years, was a stalwart lad. He stood above six feet, and was built proportionately. The sailors laughed at him when he demanded payment and a struggle followed. By exerting his powerful strength and some resourcefulness, Jack succeeded in overcoming the crew.

It was then that he learned there were two prisoners aboard the ship. These he released. They proved to be Frank Chadwick and a British secret diplomatic agent.

Frank, who had been in Germany when the great European war broke out, had become separated from his father after getting over the border into Italy. In Naples one night he had gone to the aid of a sailor on the water front and saved him from injury at the hands of three others.

The sailor whom Frank had rescued showed a queer sense of gratitude by having him shanghaied aboard a small schooner. Here, under the stern rule of an American skipper, he had become one of the crew. The crew mutinied, killed the captain, and, binding Frank securely, threw him below with the other prisoner, the diplomatic agent.

Jack's unexpected appearance upon the scene was indeed a welcome sight to both. Upon learning the nature of the work upon which the secret agent was bound, the two lads had volunteered to help him out. This offer was accepted, and thus both found themselves principal figures in a diplomatic coup that broke up the Triple Alliance and took the support of Italy away from Germany and Austria.

It was while with the secret agent that they had met Lord Hastings, and it was through the good offices of the latter that they finally found themselves attached to the British fleet as midshipmen. Lord Hastings had taken an instant liking to the lads and had them attached to his ship. Later they had been commissioned lieutenants.

Jack and Frank had seen considerable fighting. It was through their strategy that the British had won their first sea victory, off the coast of Heligoland, when four of Germany's most powerful sea fighters had been sent to the bottom. They had saved the British fleet from possible annihilation by being fortunate to discover a spy.

The two lads, since the war began, had seen service in many waters. They had been on patrol duty off the west coast of Africa; they had served under the French flag when, under the tricolor, they had delivered a severe blow to the Austrian fleet in the Adriatic; they had trailed the German cruiser Emden, nicknamed the "terror of the sea," through the Indian ocean, and had been present when she was finally sunk by the Australian cruiser Sydney; they had taken part in sinking the German fleet in the South Atlantic, off the Falkland islands; they had been aboard a British submarine that sank three Turkish cruisers in the Persian Gulf; they had seen the capture of the German fortress of Tsing-Tau, in China, by allied British and Japanese troops, and finally they had been instrumental, while in London, of exposing a plot that would have been a severe blow to Great Britain, and of capturing a second German spy and a British traitor, who stood high in the regard of Winston Spencer Churchill, first lord of the Admiralty.

6

Three times the ships to which they were attached had been sunk, and they had had many narrow escapes. Once Lord Hastings had gone down with their vessel, and the lads had believed him drowned, but he escaped and they encountered him weeks later.

When their last craft had been sunk, upon the boys' suggestion, Lord Hastings had requested command of a submarine, and when they had once again set forth, it was in the D-16.

And as the D-16 was something absolutely new in the way of submarines, a few words concerning it are necessary here.

CHAPTER II.
THE D-16.

The British submarine D-16 was, at this time at any rate, the only under-the-water vessel that could remain under the sea indefinitely. The one real weakness of beneath-the-sea fighters had always been their inability to remain long under water, and for this reason they could operate only within a certain radius of their base.

In discovering that there was a means by which a submarine could remain indefinitely under water, Sir John H— — had overcome this difficulty. The new invention had been tried on the D-16, and it had worked.

According to Sir John, a submarine in order to remain submerged indefinitely, must be able to extract air from the water, as does a fish, for it is air that is needed most under water. Up to the time of Sir John H— —'s discovery this had never been accomplished.

Reasoning that it must be a peculiarity about the gills of a fish that permitted it to extract air from the water, Sir John had experimented along this line, and his experiments finally terminated successfully. When the D-16 had proved the practicability of Sir John's theory, the vessel had immediately been put into commission, and the construction of others begun.

The secret of the D-16 was known to only a trusted few besides the crew of the vessel—the King, Winston Churchill, and David Lloyd George, Chancellor of the Exchequer. Besides her ability to remain submerged, D-16 was also many knots faster than any other submarine.

From a naval viewpoint, perhaps, the war up to this time had not progressed as favorably as had been expected. While the allied forces on the continent had been hemming in the Germans and their allies, driving them back from beneath the very walls of Paris, back across the Marne and across the Aisne, and while the legions of the Czar had been attempting to force a passage of the Carpathian mountains for an invasion of Hungary and Austria, and making determined assault within the borders of East Prussia, the British, French and Russian fleets had been practically inactive.

True, there had been several important naval battles, but none which could be called decisive, although whatever advantage there was was with the British.

The French, with the Austrian fleet cooped up in their base in the Adriatic, had little to do but to see that the Austrians were not allowed to escape. The Russian fleet had had one or two brushes with the Turks, but these were unimportant.

In the North Sea England was having more difficulty. German submarines, from their base at Ostend, had made several successful raids into Dover harbor, on the British coast; three unfortified towns on the coast had been razed by German shells and German aeroplanes had been seen flying about in the vicinity of London.

Huge Zeppelin balloons, upon which, England believed, the German Emperor planned to risk all should other means fail, had been seen over the British Isles, but had been driven off. One had been sunk. After this, England, ever fearful of an air raid, took heart, and agreed with the nobleman who said that a raid by air was not feasible.

Besides the ships of war that had been sunk by the Germans, British merchant vessels had also been sent to the bottom by the enemy's submarines.

But the main German fleet was cooped up in Heligoland and in the Kiel canal by the British blockade, which, in itself, was proof positive of Great Britain's naval supremacy. The Kaiser had no mind to give open battle to England on the sea.

This was the situation, then, when submarine D-16 set forth from London, to do, with her new power, what damage she could to the enemy's fleet.

One day, while the lads had been looking over the vessel, as she lay in drydock, they had seen a man run furtively from the place as they approached; but they were unable to catch him. A second time they had seen him, though not close enough to identify him.

Although both had thought considerably of the matter, neither had mentioned it to the other, and it had been allowed to drop. Nor had they come upon the man again before they put to sea.

The sinking of the German vessel related in the first chapter had been the first venture of the D-16, and now the vessel was heading toward the coast of England again, having gone as far toward the strong fortress of Heligoland as Lord Hastings had deemed advisable at that time.

All day the little vessel continued on her way, traveling upon the surface, for there was now no need to submerge. She went very slowly, and night found her not many miles from the scene of her first encounter.

A sharp lookout was kept for some sign of an enemy, but there was none.

With the coming of the first light of day, Jack and Frank ascended the bridge together, and turned their eyes toward the west. A faint cloud of smoke on the horizon gave evidence of a ship of some sort.

"Probably a British vessel," said Jack.

"Can't tell," returned Frank. "A German cruiser may have succeeded in running the blockade and getting in behind."

"That's true, too," Jack agreed. "It's a mystery to me how they do it. England is supposed to have them safely bottled up. It's beyond me how they get out."

"It's beyond me, too. Of course, it's easy enough for the submarine; but you'd think we'd be bound to spot a big cruiser."

"Something will have to be done, sooner or later. What's the use of a blockade if it doesn't blockade?"

"Well," said Frank dryly, "I have no doubt that if you have a plan, the admiralty would be glad to know it."

"I haven't any plan; but England will have to do something. That's certain."

"There is no question about that. Hello!"

"What's up?" asked Jack, looking at his friend in some surprise.

For answer Frank pointed toward the east. Jack peered intently into the distance and also uttered an exclamation of surprise.

"Germans?" he asked.

"Must be," replied Frank briefly.

He glanced ahead again. Then turned to his friend with an exclamation of satisfaction.

"If they are," he said, "they'll get more than they bargained for this time."

For what his eyes had made out, through his glass, was the outline of five large battle cruisers, convoyed by a flotilla of torpedo boats.

"British?" asked Jack eagerly.

"Look like it," replied Frank, "but I can't tell for sure."

It was plain to both lads that neither fleet had made out the presence of the other, and both—the one from the West and the one from the East—were steaming directly toward the little submarine, which lay squarely between them, though out of sight, because she sat so low in the water.

"Call Lord Hastings," said Jack, and Frank hastened to obey.

A moment later the commander of the D-16 appeared on the bridge. He took in the situation at a glance.

"The fleet to the east is German," he said, after a careful scrutiny through his glass, "and the other must be the British fleet commanded by Admiral Beatty."

"Then there will be a fight," said Frank.

"There will be unless the Germans perceive our ships soon enough to give them a chance to escape," returned Lord Hastings. "Another hour undiscovered, however, and we'll get them sure, for if I am not mistaken, the leading British ships are the Lion and the Tiger—the fastest cruisers afloat today. Also their guns are greatly superior to those of the enemy."

"But what are we going to do?" asked Frank, somewhat impatiently. "We are not going to stand by and look on, are we?"

11

Lord Hastings smiled.

"Don't you worry," he said quietly. "We'll take our part, whatever it may be. We'll go below now."

The three descended. The conning tower and bridge were closed behind them, and soon the tanks were opened. The D-16 submerged until the top of her periscope barely protruded above the edge of the water.

Lord Hastings, Frank and Jack took turns watching the approach of the two fleets, now that they were in range of the periscope; and it was while the latter was at the instrument that sudden signs of commotion became noticeable on the German vessels. At the same instant Jack perceived that the British ships had increased their stride, and were making directly for the Germans.

"They have sighted each other, sir," he cried, turning to Lord Hastings in great excitement.

Lord Hastings sprang to the periscope.

"And the Germans are turning to run," he said, after a quick glance.

It was true. The German commander, realizing that he was probably no match for the powerful British squadron, had no mind to give battle when the odds were as nearly even as they were now. Evidently he had more confidence in the power of his enemy than he had in his own. Therefore, immediately the British fleet was sighted, he gave the command to come about and make for the protection of the mined area about Heligoland at full speed.

But the time lost in coming about was to prove a severe blow to the Germans. The British fleet, led by the Tiger, Admiral Beatty's flagship, had sighted its prey, and was making after it at full speed.

"Guess we might as well take a hand in this," remarked Lord Hastings coolly. "Submerge another five fathoms, Mr. Templeton."

More water was let into the tanks and the D-16 dropped rapidly lower into the sea.

"Full speed ahead, Mr. Templeton," came the next command.

The D-16 seemed to leap forward like a live thing, as she dashed in pursuit of the fleeing German fleet.

"More notches for the table, I guess," said Frank to Jack.

"We'll see," was the latter's reply. "I hope so."

CHAPTER III.

THE ENGAGEMENT.

Meanwhile the British fleet, consisting of five first-class battle cruisers, together with a flotilla of perhaps twenty torpedo boat destroyers, was steaming rapidly in pursuit of the fleeing enemy.

The German fleet, while not as powerful as the British, nevertheless presented a formidable array of fighting ships. Three first-class battle cruisers and one second-class battle cruiser and a torpedo boat flotilla greater than that of the English were in line, and it seemed to Frank and Jack that the odds were nearly enough equal for the German commander to give battle.

However, such was not the enemy's plan; for, once having turned tail to the British, the German ships put on full speed and made as fast as possible for the protection of the German mine field which protected the entrance to Heligoland. It became evident that the enemy would fight only as a last resort.

The British fleet was in full chase. First came the Tiger, the flagship of Admiral Beatty. Next in line was the Lion, a cruiser of the same class, and behind these followed three other powerful English cruisers.

At a command from the flagship, the British torpedo boats headed in the direction of the German ships of the same class, which had borne off a trifle to the north.

So far not a shot had been fired, for the British had not yet drawn close enough to the flying enemy to be within range. Half an hour passed, an hour, and then the great forward turret guns of the Tiger opened upon the rear German ship, which proved to be the Bluecher, a cruiser of the second class.

The first shot went wide, and the second. But with the third shot the British gunners found the range, and a shell dropped squarely upon the bridge of the Bluecher. A veritable cloud of steel and débris of all sorts rose high in the air above the Bluecher, and, falling, showered death among the crew.

A second and a third well-directed shell struck the Bluecher amidships and staggered her. She reeled like a drunken man, seemed about to roll over on her side, then righted herself and steamed on, but slower than before.

Now the Tiger, the first British ship, was upon her; but the Tiger did not stop. She had no time to waste on the Bluecher, already wounded unto death. As she steamed majestically past, however she poured a broadside into the reeling ship; then sped on in pursuit of the other enemies.

Now the Lion also came abreast of the Bluecher, and she, too, as she passed, poured in a broadside. It was more than the sinking Bluechercould stand. One last shot she hurled toward the Tiger, and almost before the British vessel had drawn away from her, she reeled once more and disappeared beneath the sea. As she did so, her crew hurled themselves into the water.

Now the Lion and Tiger had drawn within range of the other German cruisers and their huge shells were raining death and ruin upon them. Suddenly the rear German ship burst into flames, and her pace slackened.

Flushed with success, and with victory within their grasp, the British sailors raised a loud cheer, and the British guns spoke oftener and with greater effect than before.

But the Germans had not been idle. Outranged by the British as they were, they had opened with their great guns the moment the British had come within range. One shell raked the forward deck of the Tiger, and carried away a part of the turret, killing several men. A second struck theLion, wounding several officers and a number of sailors, though none was killed on the second ship.

Now, with victory almost in their hands, the British fleet, at a signal from the flagship, gave up the chase and fell back. Only the Bluecherhad been sunk, though two of the enemy's remaining three cruisers were in flames and the third had been badly damaged.

A cry of dismay went up from the British when the order to slow down was given. For the moment the men were at a loss to account for this action, and the officers of the various ships themselves were, for the moment, disappointed.

But Admiral Beatty had acted wisely. Ten minutes' further steaming and the Germans had entered the protection of the mine field, where it would have been death for the British to have followed without a map of the mined area. Admiral Beatty's action in calling off his fleet was given at the right moment, for had the British followed the chase would have ended disastrously.

When the German cruiser Bluecher had disappeared beneath the waves, the crew of one of the British cruisers had manned the boats and was endeavoring to save the lives of the Germans who had leaped into the water.

Almost two hundred of them had been picked up. Suddenly, right in the spot where the British sailors were engaged in the work of rescue, a torpedo flashed by with a sharp hiss. Had it struck one of the boats, all near must have been killed. A second followed closely after the first, and the British were forced to give up the work of rescue, for to have remained in the spot would have been to invite certain death.

Thus, by firing at British sailors engaged in the task of saving surviving German sailors, a German submarine had been the means of losing several score of German lives.

Meanwhile what of the British submarine D-16, which, before the battle commenced, was bearing Frank and Jack swiftly toward the German fleet?

Beneath the water, Lord Hastings had no way of determining what was going on above. The D-16 had submerged until her periscope was of no value, but Lord Hastings had deemed this advisable, because, had the periscope been allowed to protrude above water, it might have been carried away by a German shell.

Now the D-16, besides being able to remain under water indefinitely, had as before stated an added superiority over other under-the-sea-fighters, for she was able, when pushed to the limit, to make a speed of thirty knots — a speed much greater even than that of any of the cruisers above her.

Therefore, when the British fleet came within range of the enemy, the D-16 was far in advance of her fellows, under the water.

"We'll leave the big fellows to settle with the German cruisers," said Lord Hastings calmly. "We'll try our luck with the torpedo boats."

Jack and Frank nodded that they understood and approved of the plan.

"I guess the big fellows can take care of them all right," replied Frank dryly.

"They always have been able to," agreed Jack.

When, finally, Lord Hastings judged that they must be in close proximity to the German torpedo flotilla, he ordered that the D-16 rise until her periscope showed them their surroundings. Then, as he viewed the scene about him, he stepped quickly back and ordered:

"Submerge!"

Instantly the D-16 dived, and Lord Hastings turned to the two lads.

"I didn't calculate just right," he told them. "We went up right in the midst of the enemy."

"Did they see us?" asked Jack anxiously.

"I don't know. However, I have the range. Have the men stand by the torpedoes."

The men sprang quickly to their posts at Jack's command, and then Lord Hastings gave the order to rise slowly.

Slowly the water was forced from the tanks once more, and gradually the submarine arose, until her periscope once more protruded just above the water.

"No. 2 torpedo!" ordered Lord Hastings. "Ready?"

"Aye, aye, sir," came the reply of the man, who stood almost at his commander's elbow, and therefore could plainly hear the command.

For the others, further away, it would be necessary to use the signal board.

"Fire!" cried Lord Hastings.

17

A sharp metallic click was the only answer, and all on board stood quiet. Lord Hastings kept his eye glued to the periscope.

Then those on board saw him throw up his hand with a gesture of satisfaction, and none needed to be told that the torpedo had gone true.

Now the attention of all was given to the signal board, at Lord Hastings' side. The men stood at their posts, as did Frank and Jack, awaiting the signal that would mean the firing of another torpedo.

There was not a sound to break the stillness other than the purr of the engine. But the stillness could only be termed such because there were no regular noises. In spite of this a voice could be heard but a few feet away, because of the heavy pressure of the water above.

Suddenly the signal board flashed red. The men read:

"No. 3 torpedo! No. 4 torpedo!"

Lord Hastings had decided upon a bold stroke. He had determined to deliver a double blow to the enemy before he was forced to submerge, to escape the fire of the enemy.

He gauged the range for each torpedo, and this was flashed upon the signal board. Then came the next command:

"Attention!"

Eagerly, though quietly, the men awaited the next command. There was not a nervous hand aboard. All bore themselves with the easy nonchalance that has been the character of the British sailor through all the ages; but their fingers twitched with impatience.

And then the signal board again glowed in burning letters:

"Fire!"

"Click! Click!"

Not another sound, and even these only audible to the men who had launched the torpedoes, and two powerful engines of destruction, aimed true, sped on the errand of death and disaster.

At the same moment the signal board flashed:

CHAPTER IV.
A DARING PLAN.

Jack stepped to Lord Hastings' side and shouted:

"Did we get 'em?"

Lord Hastings shook his head.

"I don't know," he replied. "We'll go up again directly."

He ordered the submarine to proceed ahead half a mile, and then rise.

This was done, and as the periscope once more took in the sight about, Lord Hastings, who gazed through it, stepped quickly aside and motioned to Jack to peer in. The lad did so, and stepped back with an exclamation of delight.

Frank also peered into the periscope, and uttered an exclamation of pleasure as his eyes took in the scene about.

Speeding forward in the wake of the German cruisers, which the periscope made plain, were all the German torpedo boats, except three. These lay helpless upon the surface of the sea, and it was plainly evident that they were settling rapidly.

Their crews were hurriedly getting out the small boats, and jumping overboard. The D-16 had done her work well.

Frank turned away from the periscope.

"Three notches in the table," he said to Jack, who stood at his side.

"Right," replied the latter briefly.

Feeling perfectly secure now, Lord Hastings ordered that the submarine be brought to the surface, and followed by Frank and Jack, he stepped out on the bridge.

They stepped out just in time to see the sinking of the Bluecher by the British cruiser Lion, and from their posts they watched the chase of the others. Frank and Jack were greatly surprised when the British admiral signalled for his ships to draw off.

"Great Scott!" exclaimed Frank. "He had them right in his hands. Why didn't he follow 'em up?"

"It's too deep for me," said Jack, in some disgust.

"Come, come," said Lord Hastings. "You must give the Admiral credit for having some sense, you know."

"Then why did he do it?" questioned Frank.

"Why," said Lord Hastings, "because, had he followed another mile, the entire British fleet might have been sent to the bottom."

"What do you mean?" asked Jack.

"Mines," replied Lord Hastings. "The enemy has reached the protection of his mine field."

"I see," said Frank, somewhat taken aback. "Of course. I should have known that the Admiral had some good reason for not following up his advantage."

"You let your feelings get away with you sometimes," said Lord Hastings.

"Well, I'll promise not to do so any more," said Frank.

"I wouldn't make any rash promises, if I were you," said Jack, with a smile.

"Well, I mean it," said Frank.

"Oh, well, if you mean it, all right. Only you are liable to forget yourself if you are not careful."

Jack turned to Lord Hastings.

"Which way now, sir?" he asked.

Lord Hastings was silent for some moments, but said finally:

"I guess we might as well cruise about here. Some of these other fellows are likely to come sneaking out, and we may nab them."

"If you please, sir," said Frank, "I believe I have a better plan than that."

"Let's have it," said his commander briefly.

"Well," said Frank, "these German submarines have been making raids on the coast of England. What's the matter with our doing a little of that kind of work?"

"By Jove!" said Jack. "A good idea. What do you say, sir?" turning to Lord Hastings.

Lord Hastings was plainly undecided. It was evident that he looked with some favor upon the plan, but he hesitated, not because of fear, but rather because he was not entirely certain that it could be accomplished successfully.

"Where would you plan to make an attack?" he asked of Frank.

"Why, right in Heligoland, sir."

"But the mines?"

Frank shrugged his shoulders.

"The Germans don't pay much attention to our mines," he said.

"Well, no, they don't, that's true," agreed Lord Hastings.

"Besides," said Jack, "we can go beneath the mines."

"I guess we could do that," agreed Lord Hastings. "While we cannot tell just where the mines lay, we have, nevertheless, a first-class map of Heligoland and the sea surrounding, and by paying careful attention we may be able to get through safely."

"Then we shall make the attempt, sir?" asked Frank eagerly.

Lord Hastings smiled.

"Yes," he said quietly.

"Good!" cried Jack and Frank in a single voice.

"It has always seemed strange to me," said Frank, "why such an attempt has not been made before. The Germans do it. Why haven't we?"

"Well," said Lord Hastings, "I suppose the main reason is that Heligoland is too far away."

"But the Germans have done it," said Jack.

"True; but you must remember they have established a naval base at Ostend; and the distance from Ostend to Dover, and other British coast towns, is not as great as from the British coast to Heligoland."

"I hadn't thought of that," said Frank. "However, I know this much. In every war in which the United States has engaged, some such desperate attempt has resulted successfully. Take Dewey at Manila, or Farragut at Mobile Bay. Both went right in, regardless of mines and forts."

"That is true," said Lord Hastings. "No one can dispute the bravery and daring of the American sailor. Nevertheless, it has always seemed to me to be foolhardy. Had it been absolutely necessary, it would have been different. But a blockade would have been just as effective."

"I don't know about that," replied Frank. "Ever since the beginning of this war I have wondered why a British fleet didn't try to get at the Germans."

"Well, as nearly as I can make out," said Lord Hastings, "it is because it has been believed unnecessary to take such a chance."

"Of course," said Frank, "we, in this submarine, will have a better chance of performing such a raid successfully than any other vessel, because we can go beneath the water, and stay there until we get ready to come up."

"Right you are," agreed Jack. "All we have to do is to figure the distance from here to a point where, being sure it is not mined, we wish to rise. Then, calculating our speed, we shall know just when to come up safely."

"Perfectly simple," said Lord Hastings with a smile, "if we don't hit a mine before we get there."

"Don't you think, sir, that by going beneath the mines we will be successful?"

"If I didn't I wouldn't make the attempt," said Lord Hastings dryly. "I remember how you did it when you sank that Turkish cruiser in the Dardanelles."

"And had we had this vessel at our disposal," said Jack, "we could have done considerable more damage. As it was we had to get back before we exhausted our air supply."

"We have an advantage in that respect. There can be no question about that," said Lord Hastings.

"Well, when shall we start, sir?" asked Frank.

"Immediately," was the reply.

The three turned their eyes over the sea to where the British fleet, retiring, could be seen moving toward the west. One of the large cruisers, the Tiger, was being towed by a torpedo boat.

"Hope she is not badly damaged," said Jack, noticing how the British cruiser staggered.

"She looks fit enough," said Frank.

"The trouble is you can never tell by the looks," said Lord Hastings. "However, I guess she is in no danger of sinking."

"Let us hope her death list is small," said Jack fervently.

"Let us hope so," agreed Lord Hastings. "Come, we may as well go below."

The commander of the D-16 descended from the bridge and the lads followed him.

"We may as well submerge here," said Lord Hastings, "for every foot we advance on the surface of the water is putting us in the way of hitting a German mine. We can't be too careful."

"But it is hardly likely there would be any about here, sir," said Frank.

"Have you forgotten what it was that caused Admiral Beatty to give up the pursuit of the enemy?" asked Lord Hastings.

"That's so, sir," said Frank. "I had forgotten."

"Besides," said Jack, "the Germans may have dropped more mines to cover their retreat."

"Exactly," said Lord Hastings.

"Well, let's dive then," said Frank.

"The sooner the better it will suit me," said Jack.

"So be it then," from Lord Hastings. "You may give the order, Mr. Templeton."

Jack obeyed, and slowly, as the water was let into her tanks, the D-16 sank and sank, until, certain that she was beneath the enemy's mines, Lord Hastings gave the command: "Full speed ahead!"

CHAPTER V.
TROUBLE ON BOARD.

"It's as well to go quickly," Lord Hastings said, giving his reason for ordering full speed ahead. "I hardly anticipate they have mined very deep here. We'll slow down further along."

"If we bump a mine," said Frank, "I can't see that it will make any difference whether we are going fast or slowly."

"It won't make much," agreed Jack dryly.

According to Lord Hastings' calculations, which proved to be correct, they were now off the coast of Holland.

Several hours passed, and then, at Lord Hastings' command, the solid glass front of the submarine was plunged into utter darkness and the powerful searchlight brought to bear on the water ahead, while, at the same time, the speed was reduced to seven knots.

In spite of its powerfulness, the searchlight lighted up the water for only a short distance ahead, and, as Lord Hastings said, should a mine be seen ahead prompt action would be necessary to save them from disaster.

Frank took his place just behind the searchlight, while the compartment behind was closed that no light might enter from without, thus adding a little to the effect of the searchlight.

His watch was set for two hours, and he had sat most of that time with eyes straight ahead, when he became conscious that the door behind him was being pushed slowly open.

Certain in his own mind that his watch was not up, and mindful of Lord Hastings' order that the door be not opened unless absolutely necessary, Frank nevertheless did not take his eyes off the sea ahead, but called out:

"Who's there? What is it?"

There was no answer.

"Something wrong," muttered the lad to himself, and acted upon the instant.

Through the little tube at his elbow he shouted a command:

"Stop her!"

At the same moment, even as he felt the sudden shock as the submarine paused abruptly in her pace, he sprang from his seat and turned toward the door, ready for anything with one hand on his automatic, for he felt sure that he was in danger.

In the darkness behind he could see nothing, but the slight squeaking of a board gave evidence of another presence. Frank, with the searchlight behind, was in full view of the other, and the lad realized it.

With a quick backward leap he snapped off the searchlight, and then dropped quickly to the floor, even as a figure rushed toward him in the darkness.

Frank's ruse undoubtedly stood him to good advantage. A foot struck his prostrate body, and the figure of a man pitched over him, muttering a fierce imprecation as he fell to the floor.

Before the latter could rise, Frank grappled with him. Quickly reversing his revolver, he brought the butt of the weapon down in the direction in which he judged the man's head to be. It struck something soft, and a guttural howl of pain went up.

"A spy!" Frank found time to think to himself.

But he had not struck the man's head, only a hand which had been outstretched, and before he could draw his pocket searchlight to ascertain what damage he had done, the lad felt a pair of arms about his neck, and a hand seeking to entwine itself in his throat.

His revolver he found now to be of no use, so he dropped it and struck out blindly with his bare fists. Once, twice, his fists found their mark, and each time a blow went home the lad was rewarded by hearing cries of pain from his opponent.

As the two struggled, there flashed before the lad a vision of a man running from where the D-16 lay in drydock some days before.

"I guess we have got him at last," the lad muttered between his teeth, and putting all his force behind one more blow, he struck out savagely.

The arms about his neck relaxed their pressure and the man sank to the floor while Frank felt the form grow limp beneath him.

The lad stood up and walked across the little room to snap on the searchlight.

As he did so the man on the floor came quickly to his feet, and before Frank could stop him, had darted from the room and disappeared. Through the door he left open streamed a faint light.

Frank sprang after the retreating figure with a cry of anger. Dashing out of the door he bumped squarely into the figure of another man advancing toward him. Without pausing to see who the newcomer might be, Frank grappled with him.

"Here, here, what's the meaning of this?" asked a well-known voice, and Frank released his hold and stepped back.

The newcomer was Lord Hastings.

"What's the matter with you?" asked the commander of the vessel. "Have you gone crazy? I stopped the ship in response to your command and when I asked you, through the tube, what was wrong I didn't get an answer. And now you jump on me. What's the matter?"

"Spy aboard, sir," replied Frank briefly.

"What!" exclaimed Lord Hastings, starting back.

"Spy aboard, sir," repeated Frank.

"Impossible!" exclaimed Lord Hastings. "Have you lost your senses? How could a spy have got aboard?"

"As to that I don't know," replied the lad, "but nevertheless there is a spy aboard. I'll stake my life on that."

Then he proceeded to relate what had occurred.

Lord Hastings grew very grave. He took Frank by the arm.

"Come with me," he said quietly.

He led the way to his own cabin, where he passed the word for Jack. The latter arrived almost immediately, and the situation was explained to him.

"I believe," said Frank, "that the man is the same I saw lurking about the ship yard before the D-16 was put into commission.

"So you saw him, too?" exclaimed Jack.

"Yes, I saw him, but I didn't know you did," replied Frank.

"I didn't say anything because I thought I must be wrong," said Jack. "It didn't seem possible a German spy could have gained admittance there."

"Just what I thought," said Frank.

"Do you suppose the man who attacked you just now is one of the crew?" asked Lord Hastings.

"Who else could he be, sir?"

"But I could have sworn by the members of my crew. They have all been in the service for years and are British to the backbone."

"There must be one who isn't," said Frank, "for when I struck him he let out a stream of German oaths."

"Would you recognize him?"

"I am afraid not. It was perfectly dark, and I didn't even get a glimpse of his face. All that I could make out was that he was a big man."

"We have several big men in the crew," said Lord Hastings.

"But," said Frank suddenly, "I might be able to identify him if I got a look at his hand."

"Why?"

"I hit him with my revolver butt. I thought it was his head but it must have been his hand."

Lord Hastings, who had been seated, stood up.

"We'll see," he said.

He walked to the door and summoned the chief gunner's mate.

"Johnson," he said, "take a brace of automatics and summon every man of the crew here, coon, engineer and all. Don't let a single one get the drop on you."

Johnson looked blankly at his commander.

"Why — why — —" he stammered.

"There is a spy aboard, Johnson," said Lord Hastings calmly. "Hurry."

The old man drew himself up and touched his cap.

"Aye, aye, sir," he said quietly. "I'll bring 'em."

He turned and marched rapidly away.

"I happen to know he's not your man," said Lord Hastings with a slight smile, "for I was standing right beside him when I got your command to stop."

"We had better let Johnson line them all up outside the door, and question each man separately, sir," said Frank.

"A good suggestion," said Lord Hastings.

They sat quiet for perhaps five minutes, and then Johnson's voice came from outside.

"I've got 'em all here, sir."

Frank arose and walked out the door. There stood the full crew of the ship with arms in the air, under the muzzles of Johnson's two automatics.

"Send them in one at a time, Johnson," Frank ordered.

"Aye, aye, sir," replied the old man, and waving his revolver at one he commanded: "You first."

The first sailor was white of face and evidently badly frightened. He entered the room slowly and came to attention before Lord Hastings.

"Your name?" demanded the commander.

"Brice, sir."

"Any other name?"

"Yes, sir, Harvey, sir."

"No; I mean were you ever known by another name; an alias?"

"Well, sir," replied the sailor plainly confused, "no, sir, yes, sir. Before I enlisted I was known as Ryan, sir."

"That's hardly German," said Lord Hastings. "And why did you change your name?"

"A little trouble with the police, sir, if you must know."

At this moment Frank, who had approached closely, suddenly spoke in German.

"Your name?" he commanded.

The sailor stared at him blankly.

"He's not the one," said Jack. "His surprise is genuine enough. Call the next."

"Stand over there in the corner," said Frank to the sailor. "Jack, you keep them covered as I line them up. We must be careful."

"Send in another, Johnson," called Lord Hastings.

A second sailor appeared in the door. His right hand was wrapped in a handkerchief!

CHAPTER VI.
THE SPY.

Frank's hand dropped quickly to his revolver.

"Stand over there," he commanded in a harsh voice.

The man obeyed, and Frank approached and looked at him carefully.

"He is about the same build, sir," he said, turning to Lord Hastings.

Lord Hastings confronted the sailor.

"Your name?" he demanded.

"Thompson, sir," was the reply, and the man let fall his arms, which he had kept above his head when he entered.

Immediately Frank's revolver flashed forth.

"Hands up there, Thompson," he said quietly.

Plainly frightened, Thompson obeyed.

"How long have you been in the service?" demanded Lord Hastings.

"Ten years, sir."

"Ever known by any other name?"

"No, sir."

"Are you of German descent?"

"There is not a drop of German blood in me, so far as I know, sir."

"Do you speak German?"

"A little, sir."

Lord Hastings looked at the man closely, and demanded suddenly:

"What is the matter with your hand?"

"I was helping Smith in the engine room, sir, and a heavy block fell on it, sir."

"Let me see it."

Slowly the sailor unwrapped the bandage and exposed his hand. It was very red across the top, and Frank, glancing at it, believed that the mark could have well been caused by the blow of a revolver butt.

"I should say he is the man, sir," he said quietly to Lord Hastings.

"It would seem so," was his commander's reply, "still we must be positive." He turned again to the sailor. "Is it not true," he asked, "that only a few moments ago you attacked Mr. Chadwick, and that your wounded hand is the result of a blow from his revolver?"

The sailor looked at his commander in surprise, that seemed genuine enough.

"No, sir," he replied quietly.

"Then you deny you are a German spy?" asked Lord Hastings.

The sailor started back, and his face turned red.

"A spy, sir!" he cried. "Me a spy? Why if there is one country under the sun for which I would not turn a hand, it is Germany."

"Circumstances are much against you, in spite of your protestations of innocence," said Lord Hastings gravely.

"But Smith, the engineer, can vouch for me, sir, and so can Black, who was in the engine room when I injured my hand. Call them, sir."

"Well, I'll call them," said Lord Hastings, "but I doubt if it will do any good."

At a command from Lord Hastings the engineer and a sailor named Black were sent into the room.

Lord Hastings turned to the engineer.

"Were you in the engine room when Thompson injured his hand?" he asked.

Smith shifted uneasily from one foot to the other.

"Yes, sir," he replied at length.

"He says that a block fell on his hand. Is that true?"

"Well, sir, I—I——" stammered Smith.

"Come, sir, this is a serious matter," said Lord Hastings sternly.

"No, sir, it isn't true," said Smith. "He——"

"That is enough," said Lord Hastings. He turned to Black. "Thompson says you were there. Is it true that a block fell on his hand?"

"No, sir," said Black. "He——"

"That's enough," said Lord Hastings again. "It looks to me as if you were guilty."

"If you please, sir," said Thompson quietly, "will you allow me to ask Smith and Black one question?"

Lord Hastings nodded his head in assent.

"Smith," said Thompson, "how did I injure my hand?"

"Why," said Smith, "you miscalculated, and instead of putting it against Black's head, you put it against the door."

Thompson turned to Black.

"Is that true?" he asked.

"Yes," replied Black.

Thompson turned to Lord Hastings.

"That should be enough, sir," he said quietly.

"What is the meaning of this?" demanded Lord Hastings, looking from one to the other of the three men.

"It's plain enough," said Jack stepping forward. "Thompson and Black were settling an argument of some sort by the use of the fists. And Smith, I take it, was the referee. Am I right?"

"Right you are, sir," replied Smith. "But we didn't— —"

"Never mind, never mind," said Jack with a wave of his hand. "All of you line up there alongside Brice." He turned to Frank and Lord Hastings. "We are on the wrong track," he said.

"So it seems," replied Lord Hastings, "but appearances were against him. We'll have to look further."

One after another the members of the crew were examined, but in spite of the best efforts put forward by Lord Hastings, Jack and Frank, not one of them could be tripped up.

"But it must have been one of them," said Frank, after all had been examined and given satisfactory accounts of themselves. "It must be one of them. I certainly didn't dream I was attacked. But who was it?"

"Can there be a stowaway aboard?" asked Jack.

"I never thought of that," exclaimed Frank. "Shall I have the ship searched, sir?"

"Immediately," ordered Lord Hastings. "We'll leave Johnson here to guard these men, while we make a thorough search."

From stem to stem they searched the little submarine. Not a single movable obstacle but what they moved. It was as systematic a search as it was possible to conduct, but there was no sign of a stowaway.

"Well, there is no one here," said Frank, when the search had been concluded. "Therefore, it must have been a member of the crew."

They went back to Lord Hastings' quarters, where Johnson still stood on guard. Lord Hastings looked them over carefully, then spoke.

"Men," he said, and his voice was very grave. "Some place on this vessel there is a traitor. We have searched high and low for some sign of a stranger, but we could find no one. Therefore, the spy must be among you. Will he step forward and save his companions from the finger of suspicion?"

Not a man stirred.

"Then— —" began Lord Hastings, but he was interrupted by a sudden motion of the vessel, which seemed to be flying up through the water.

Up to this time it had been perfectly stationary.

"What's the meaning of that?" cried Lord Hastings when he had recovered his balance.

"I should say someone was forcing the water out of the tanks, sir," replied Jack calmly.

"But every man is in this room," replied the commander.

"You forget the stowaway, sir," said Frank.

"But there is no stowaway."

"There must be a stowaway! How else do you account for this? The vessel could not do it by itself."

There was still a perceptible motion of the vessel.

"We're rising," cried Jack in alarm. "Someone has tampered with the tanks. We are likely to hit a mine."

Lord Hastings turned to the sailors.

"Men," he said quickly, "until this matter has been finally settled, I must let you all go. But, each of you keep an eye on your companion, and at the first sign of treachery, shoot him. Search the ship."

He followed Frank, who had dashed toward the compartments in which were located the water tanks, by means of which the vessel rose and submerged. As he dashed forward there came to his ears the sound of a shot.

The commander of the D-16 redoubled his stride and the men, also having heard the shot, piled after him. As he passed the door to the engine room, the figure of a large man, rushing forth at that moment, struck him squarely and knocked him down.

Lord Hastings was up in a moment and had his opponent beneath him. The latter was a powerful customer, however, and had it not been for the crew, who rushed to their commander's aid at that moment, it would have fared badly with him.

But the crew, angry that they had been under suspicion, now that they believed they had found the man who was responsible for their predicament, leaped upon the man and soon had him bound securely. At that moment Frank and Jack came upon them.

"Well, I see you have him," said Frank quietly.

"Yes," replied Lord Hastings, "but what was the shot I heard?"

"Oh that," said Frank. "He took a shot at me when I came upon him as he was fooling about the tanks."

"Did he hit you."

"No; just knocked my gun out of my hands. But you see, there was a stowaway on board."

"But where on earth was he hiding?"

"I found the hiding place," said Frank quietly. "It is in the engine room, right where he could do the most damage should occasion require. He had built himself a little stage beneath the floor, where he could lie, only coming out when it was safe."

"But why hasn't he sunk us long ago? That's what I would like to know."

"I think I can answer that," said Jack. "I should say that his work was to find out the specifications of the D-16—how she attains her great speed, and how she can remain indefinitely under water. In some way word of her building must have reached the enemy. Am I right?" he asked of the prisoner.

The latter shrugged his shoulders.

"Think as you please," he said. "Whatever my work, I have failed."

"Yes, you have failed," said Lord Hastings. "And you know the penalty?"

"Yes," said the prisoner quietly, "it is death."

"Yes," repeated Lord Hastings slowly, "it is death!" Then to the men: "Guard him as you value your lives."

Motioning to Jack and Frank to follow him, Lord Hastings led the way to his cabin.

CHAPTER VII.
DEATH OF THE SPY.

"What will you do with the spy, Lord Hastings?" asked Frank.

"Shoot him," was the brief reply.

Frank was silent for some moments.

"It's terrible to think of it," he said at last. "Still, I suppose it must be done."

"It must," returned Lord Hastings.

"Will there be need of a trial first, sir?"

"A trial, of course, is only a formality. Nevertheless, he must have one."

"When, sir?"

"The court martial will sit in half an hour."

"And will be composed of how many, sir?"

"Six. Mr. Templeton, yourself, Johnson, Smith, one of the sailors and myself. It will sit here in my cabin."

"Very good, sir. I shall be here."

Half an hour later the prisoner faced his judges. Lord Hastings addressed him.

"Prisoner," he said, "what have you to say in extenuation of your actions?"

"Nothing," was the brief response.

"Have you anything to plead why sentence of death should not be pronounced on you?" continued Lord Hastings.

"I have nothing whatever to say," was the firm response.

The six judges consulted together for some moments. Then Lord Hastings turned again to the prisoner.

"As president of this court martial," he said slowly, "I sentence you to be shot at six o'clock."

He drew a watch from his pocket and glanced at it.

"It is now five," he said. "You have one hour in which to prepare yourself to meet your maker."

The prisoner bowed his head in assent. Then, at a signal, he arose and was conducted from the room.

Six o'clock came all too swiftly for Frank and Jack, who could but look with horror upon this cold blooded way of disposing of a man, simply because he was a spy.

The D-16, feeling her way carefully, had come to the surface, and now the prisoner was conducted to the bridge. He took his stand at one end and waving aside a proffered bandage, faced his executioners unflinchingly.

A firing squad of six men took their positions opposite him. Much to his chagrin, Jack had been put in command of the squad, and it was his duty to give the word that would snuff out the life of a fellow being.

But Jack was not the lad to refuse to obey orders, and now he stood behind the squad.

"Ready," he said calmly.

"Take aim!"

But before he could give the word to fire, the prisoner, who up to this moment had been standing with folded arms, suddenly flung himself into the sea.

"Fire!" cried Jack, and the sailors poured a volley after him. Then all rushed to the rail and watched for him to reappear.

A few minutes later a head appeared a short distance away. It became at once apparent that the spy had not been touched.

Immediately Jack rushed to the side of the vessel and also flung himself into the sea. The erstwhile prisoner saw his action and struck out vigorously toward the south, where, in the gathering darkness, he could make out dimly a strip of land.

But Jack was a powerful swimmer and gained rapidly on the spy.

Perceiving that he could not out-swim his pursuer, the spy slackened his stroke, and just as Jack came up to him, dived. As he went down, he caught Jack by the legs and pulled him under also.

Taken at a disadvantage Jack struggled in vain to free himself. He was at a further disadvantage also, for the spy, before going under, had caught a long breath; whereas Jack had gone under sputtering and gasping.

But help came to Jack from a source he did not expect. When he had jumped into the sea in pursuit of the spy, Frank had done likewise, for he divined that Jack might have trouble recapturing the prisoner. While he was not such a powerful swimmer as Jack, he was nevertheless close at hand when the spy pulled his chum under.

Frank acted without an instant's hesitation. Drawing his revolver and grasping it by the barrel, he also dived. Down and down he went, and then close beside him he became aware of the struggling figures.

The water was very dark, but the lad could dimly distinguish the form of his friend from that of the spy. Going close, he raised his revolver and brought it down on the spy's head with all his force. At the same time he stretched forth his other hand, and seized the spy by the shoulder.

Freed of the hold on his legs, Jack immediately shot to the surface, where he filled his lungs with fresh invigorating air. A moment later Frank, still grasping the spy by the shoulder, appeared by his side.

"Lend a hand," he called, "and we'll get him back aboard."

Jack, now greatly refreshed, did as his chum ordered and the two lads, supporting the body of the spy between them, swam back to the submarine, where willing hands helped them over the side.

Lord Hastings immediately took charge of the spy.

"Stretch him out there till he recovers consciousness, and then proceed with the execution," he ordered.

The body of the spy was stretched out on the deck, and two sailors bent over him. Then one started back, and took off his cap.

"The execution will not take place," he said.

"What do you mean?" said Lord Hastings. "Is he — —"

"Yes," interrupted the sailor, "he is dead."

"By George!" muttered Frank, "that blow over the head."

"No," said the sailor, "it is the water that did for him."

"I'm glad of that," said Frank simply.

"Prepare the body for burial immediately," ordered Lord Hastings. "We'll remain on the surface until after he has been buried, then we'll submerge and continue our course."

The work of preparing the spy's body for burial was only a question of minutes, and when it had been turned over to the mercies of the sea, Lord Hastings gave the command:

"Submerge immediately, Mr. Templeton."

All descended from the bridge, the little vessel was made snug and comfortable, and disappeared from the surface of the sea.

"Shape your course due east, Mr. Templeton, and steam at 7 knots," ordered Lord Hastings. "Mr. Chadwick, you will take your post and watch for mines."

"Very good, sir," replied both lads, and departed on their respective duties.

In the darkened room in the bow of the vessel, with the powerful searchlight lighting up the murky water ahead, Frank kept careful vigil. Hour after hour he sat there in silence, hardly moving from his first position.

The D-16 forged ahead but slowly, for there was no need of undue haste and Lord Hastings was not minded to take unnecessary chances.

Frank glanced at his watch.

"Midnight," he muttered to himself. "Only one more hour and then I can turn in for the night."

Still the minutes passed without incident. Finally, at a few minutes to one, Frank, after a second glance at his watch, arose and stretched himself.

"Guess nothing will turn up in my watch," he told himself.

But the lad was mistaken.

For one moment he had taken his eyes from the water ahead, and now, glancing forth once more, he beheld a sight that moved him to instant action. His eyes fell upon a large object directly ahead, a scant hundred yards.

Quickly the lad jumped to the bell that signalled the engine room. And almost as quickly the speed of the vessel was checked. But the nose of the submarine was now but inches from the dark looking object ahead.

Lord Hastings' face appeared in the room.

"What's the matter?" he demanded.

"Looks like a mine, sir," replied Frank quietly.

Lord Hastings advanced until he could get a good look at the object. He peered at it long and carefully, then turned to the lad.

"You are right," he said. "It is a mine. Had you perceived it an instant later we undoubtedly would be in the land of the missing by this time."

Frank flushed at this, for he realized perfectly that had he been paying strict attention to his duties, the submarine would not have come this close to danger of destruction. But he said nothing.

The mine extended well up toward the surface of the water, but the bottom of it was in plain sight.

"I suppose the best thing to do is to dive under it," said Lord Hastings.

"My idea, too, sir," agreed Frank.

Lord Hastings turned on his heel and left the compartment, and a moment later the vessel began to sink lower and lower into the sea. Frank still stood on watch, and when he was certain that the D-16 would pass beneath the mine without danger of striking it, he gave the signal and the vessel headed forward once more.

Lord Hastings entered the compartment again.

"The chances are there are more of them," he said, "so we shall have to be very careful. I'll have Mr. Templeton take the next watch, for we cannot keep too sharp a lookout."

Frank nodded his head in assent. Lord Hastings left.

Five minutes later Jack appeared at Frank's side and the latter turned to go. Suddenly he whirled about and spoke to his chum.

"You must be more careful than I was," he said quietly. "I was almost the means of sending us all to the bottom for good."

"What do you mean?" asked Jack in surprise.

Frank explained.

"Well," said his chum consolingly, "a miss is as good as a mile, you know."

"Nevertheless," replied Frank, "the second might not be a miss. Keep your eyes open."

"I'll keep them open, never fear," said Jack. "Now, you go to bed."

"All right," said Frank, and left his friend alone.

CHAPTER VIII.

HELIGOLAND.

"Off there," said Lord Hastings, pointing over his shoulder, "lies Heligoland, one of the strongest harbors in the world, and regarded by the Kaiser and his subjects as impregnable. A raid by an enemy has been deemed as impossible by strategists."

"Nevertheless," said Frank drily, "it is not impossible, as the Kaiser and his subjects will find out."

"As I understand it," said Jack, "Heligoland is a natural stronghold."

"To a certain extent, yes," replied Lord Hastings. "Heligoland, as you know, is an island, and nature has done her best to make it immune from attack. To nature's work has been added the brains and brawn of the best German strategists and workers. An attack by a hostile battle fleet could have but one result—failure. But, so far as I have been able to determine, there as yet has been nothing devised that will ward off the attack of a submarine."

"Except mines," said Frank.

"True. But it is certain there can be no mines in the harbor proper, for they would be an eternal menace to the German fleet. Of course the entrance is strongly guarded by mines and the powerful guns of the forts. But it is our business to get beneath these and torpedo a few of the enemy's vessels before we are discovered."

"And then?" asked Jack.

"Why, then," said Lord Hastings, "we shall make off as fast as possible to return at some future date, perhaps, and pay our respects once more. As I see it, there is but one thing that is likely to cause us any trouble."

"And that, sir?" asked Frank.

"The enemy's submarines," replied his commander.

"But we have the heels of them, sir," said Jack.

"True," replied Lord Hastings, "but the trouble is we are liable to run into a net of them, and in that event we would have to fight. To my knowledge, there has never been a battle of under the sea vessels, and what the result might be it is impossible to determine."

"Well," said Frank, "we shall have to take a chance. That's all."

"That's all," agreed Lord Hastings.

Lord Hastings turned to the chart of the harbor of Heligoland and bent over it eagerly. The lads peered over his shoulder.

"We are down as deep as it is safe to go," said the commander of the submarine. "The chart shows that the water is not so very deep here, and as it is all the guide we have, we must be careful." He turned to Jack. "Proceed at five knots," he commanded.

Jack gave the necessary command, and the D-16 slowed down perceptibly.

For many minutes there was intense silence, broken at last by Lord Hastings.

"I should say," he said, "that we must now be in the harbor. I am positive we have passed under the mines safely."

"Then shall we go up, sir?" asked Frank eagerly.

Lord Hastings hesitated for a moment, and then replied:

"Yes, we may as well."

Jack took this as a command, and gave the necessary order.

Slowly the D-16 began to rise.

Lord Hastings glanced at his watch.

"Seven o'clock," he said quietly, "and there should be no moon. A good night for our work."

With the periscope barely reaching above the surface, the work of forcing water from the tanks was stopped. Lord Hastings stood quietly viewing the scene about him, and to his eyes was exposed an awesome sight.

Right in the midst of the giant German battle fleet he peered, and as he did so he could but wonder to himself that so powerful and so magnificent a fighting machine apparently had been afraid to venture forth and give battle to the fleet of England, powerful as the latter was.

The D-16, before ascending, had penetrated to the very middle of the harbor, and now that she was close to the surface, the powerful binoculars at the bottom of the periscope made clear the many vessels of the German fleet in all their majesty.

Clouds of smoke floated from their smokestacks, and this suggested something to Lord Hastings.

"Ready to set forth at any time," he muttered to himself. "Just afraid, that's all."

He stepped away from the periscope, and Jack took a turn.

"Great Scott!" he exclaimed, turning away at last. "To think that a fleet the size of that should be afraid to give battle."

"It does seem strange," said Lord Hastings.

Frank now peered into the periscope, and as he looked one of the German dreadnoughts began to move from her moorings.

"One of 'em's coming out," cried Frank. "She's headed for the open sea."

"I thought they might have determined to try a little raid when I saw all that smoke," said Lord Hastings. "We'll stop her, at any rate."

He took Frank's place at the periscope and then commanded:

"Ten knots ahead, Mr. Templeton, and prepare for action!"

Jack jumped to obey this order, and a moment later the D-16 was in fighting trim. The engines throbbed and fussed, the water parted before the sharp prow of the vessel with an angry hiss, and the men stood at their posts.

The signal board flashed its first command, in letters of fire.

"No. 1 torpedo!"

The gunner was ready, and the second command—"attention"—was scarcely necessary.

Now, through the periscope, Lord Hastings gauged the range, and the signal board showed:

"Submerge!"

Almost at the same moment a second command showed plainly.

"Fire!"

"Click!"

The first torpedo sped on its way, and at the same moment Lord Hastings shouted in Jack's ear:

"Due north, Mr. Templeton. Fifteen knots!"

The D-16 leaped ahead, and at the distance of half a mile, rose slowly to the surface.

Lord Hastings and his two officers ascended to the bridge, where they took in the scene about them with their night glasses.

In the very center of the German fleet, a huge battleship was sinking. The glare of the searchlights of the others showed her plainly to the eyes of the British. Terrified cries carried over the water. The confusion aboard the sinking vessel was terrible to behold.

Men ran hither and thither about the decks, yelling and fighting, so great was their fear. From other vessels of the fleet small boats put into the sea, to pick up those who had jumped from the wounded warship.

Suddenly there was a terrific explosion, and the German warship sprang into flames, lighting up the sky for miles around. But the D-16, in the very edge of the fiery glare, so far had been unnoticed.

"They evidently think it was an internal explosion," said Lord Hastings quietly to the two lads.

"Looks like it," replied Jack, "or they would certainly be using their searchlights to make out the presence of an enemy."

"They haven't the slightest idea an enemy could have penetrated the mined area safely," replied the commander of the submarine. "But look, she is about to go."

He pointed toward the wounded German warship. His words were true. Amidst the flashing searchlights of her sister ships, the dreadnought reared high in the air. There she poised herself for a moment; then, slowly, midst a broad circle of brilliancy, she sank, the cries of those of her crew still aboard mingling with the shouts and commands from the other ships making the night hideous.

A fierce red flame, from the top of her to the very water's edge, where it hissed loud and long, enveloped the sinking ship, as the smoke arose in a dense cloud. Came another dull explosion, and the ship split in twain. For a moment there were two distinct sheets of flame, and then the fore and aft parts of the vessel disappeared beneath the water simultaneously.

"Well, she's gone," said Lord Hastings. "Now for the next one."

"We are safe enough here, sir," said Jack, "and we are close enough to hit her. Why not fire without submerging?"

"All right," replied his commander quietly. "Order No. 2 torpedo launched immediately," and he gave the range.

Jack hastened below, only to hurry back upon the bridge again, which he reached just in time to see the second ship in the German line stagger, and sway drunkenly.

Again loud cries of fear carried across the water, and the searchlights of the still unhit German ships played upon the second wounded vessel.

"No. 3 and No. 4 torpedoes right into the midst of them!" cried Lord Hastings, and Jack jumped below to give the command.

"Click! Click!"

Two more terrible engines of destruction sped on their way.

Jack sprang back to the bridge to watch the effect of these shots.

And the effects were terrible, as the watchers could plainly make out.

Confusion reigned throughout the German fleet. Not a ship but on which there was panic, and the officers were having serious trouble with the crews.

For there could no longer be any doubt in the minds of the Germans as to the cause of the three terrific explosions that now shattered the stillness of the night.

"Boom! Boom! Boom!" they came, and showers of steel, iron, wood and débris rose high in the air, to be scattered far across the surface of the sea.

Now the searchlights of the uninjured German ships left their sinking sister ships and flashed swiftly across the water. Suddenly the D-16 was lighted up by a circle of light as bright as day.

"We are discovered!" cried Frank, and at the same moment Lord Hastings gave a command:

"Down, quick!"

He led the way through the conning tower with rapid strides, and the lads hurried after him.

"Submerge!"

A moment more and the D-16 was again beneath the sea, safe from chance German shells, and steaming toward the east.

CHAPTER IX.
A DESPERATE VENTURE.

"Which way now, sir?" asked Jack.

Lord Hastings hesitated.

"They will probably be laying for us toward the west with their submarines," he said, "and while we may be able to get by, it will be desperate work."

"Then why not go due east, sir?" asked Frank.

"The Kiel canal is due east," replied Lord Hastings.

"What of that, sir?"

"What of it? Surely, you would not suggest forcing a passage of the Kiel canal?"

"I don't see why not, sir."

Lord Hastings looked at the lad with surprise written all over his face.

"By Jove!" he said at last. "When it comes to finding ways of getting into trouble, you are the limit, as the Americans say."

"But don't you think it could be done, sir?" asked Frank.

"Well, I don't know," replied his commander. "It might be done, yes. And then again it might not. But what would be our object in getting into the Baltic?"

"Well, I understand that the Russians are having considerable trouble there," replied Frank, "and we might be able to lend them a hand."

"That's true, too," replied Lord Hastings. "I hadn't thought of that."

"Then what do you say, sir?" asked Frank.

Jack now added his voice to that of his chum, but for some moments Lord Hastings remained undecided. Frank, however, clinched the matter when he said:

"Well, there probably is no more danger that way than there is in trying to get out of here to the west, where every German submarine available is on the lookout for us."

"Besides," urged Jack, "they will watch the entrance to the Kiel canal less closely, because they would not dream of an attempt to force its passage."

"There is some truth in that, too," said Lord Hastings. "Well, the Kiel canal be it then."

Both lads were jubilant, and they could not contain themselves, but expressed their delight with loud "hurrahs" and by tossing their caps in the air.

So it came to pass that the D-16 laid herself out on a course for the Kiel canal, the waterway which the Germans had constructed at such great expense, that her fleet in the North Sea and her fleet in the Baltic might ever be in touch with one another.

An attempted passage of the Kiel canal by a hostile ship or ships had been considered out of the question by all naval authorities. Such an attempt, it was claimed, would be too foolhardy and would be bound to end in destruction.

Nevertheless, Lord Hastings, while realizing all this, was not the man to turn from a purpose once he had made up his mind. He realized the full danger of the situation much more than did Frank or Jack, who, carried away by the opportunity of participating in what would be one of the greatest naval ventures of history, had at once lost sight of all possible danger.

Deep, deep down in the sea the D-16 made her way from the harbor of Heligoland, diving far beneath the mines that protected the German fortifications. And in her wake she left three sunken German ships of war and another so badly damaged that she would be out of commission for many months.

"I am willing to bet," said Frank, "that the Germans either lay the raid to internal troubles or else claim that a British submarine flotilla of at least 20 vessels participated."

"Right you are," agreed Jack, "and they will probably add that the enemy was driven off with great loss, more than half their number being placed hors du combat."

"At the same time," interrupted Lord Hastings, "saying that 'our losses were insignificant.'"

"Well," said Frank, "I don't suppose the government can afford to let the people know just how serious their predicament is."

"That's about the size of it," agreed Lord Hastings.

The speed of the D-16, once she was beyond the German mine field, was increased to 20 knots, and she headed directly for the entrance to the Kiel canal. Frank and Jack both turned in.

With the coming of morning the D-16 was but a few miles from her goal, and Lord Hastings accordingly ordered the speed slackened that a close watch might be kept for mines.

At eight o'clock Lord Hastings checked the speed of the vessel and ordered that it be brought to the surface.

"But surely we are not through the canal yet?" protested Jack.

"No," was the reply, "but we are almost at the entrance, and I want to take a look about."

Jack did not protest further, and when the submarine again floated on the surface of the sea he followed his commander to the bridge.

There a startling sight met their gaze, for not a hundred yards away, riding gently with the even swell of the sea, lay a second submarine and she flew the Red, White and Black of Germany.

"Below quick!" cried Jack.

But Lord Hastings laid a hand on the lad's arm as he darted for the hatchway.

"Wait a minute," he said. "There doesn't seem to be any one on guard, or we should have perceived some sign of life."

The two peered long and earnestly at the German vessel, but not a sign of life could they make out.

"Must all be dead," said Jack.

"Or asleep," replied Lord Hastings.

"And that's about what's the matter," agreed Jack. "What shall we do with the boat, sink her?"

"I suppose so," replied Lord Hastings, "but I have another idea."

"What is that, sir?"

"Well, forcing a passage of the Kiel canal is bound to prove ticklish work. Now if we could lay our hands on the officer of that vessel, we might persuade him to pilot us through."

"A good idea," said Jack, "if we could only get him."

"We shall make a try at it," said his commander.

"How?" asked Jack.

For answer Lord Hastings turned and went below, and in another moment the D-16 began creeping toward the German submarine.

At a distance of only a few yards she stopped and Lord Hastings motioned to Jack to follow him, as he dropped over the side into the little launch which had been lowered into the water. To Frank he called:

"If we do not reappear on deck within ten minutes, sink her."

Frank indicated that he understood, and Lord Hastings and Jack put off for the enemy.

They clambered quietly aboard, and descended below without so much as being challenged. Just at the bottom of the companionway they came upon the figure of a man who emerged from one of the compartments. At sight of the British uniforms the man staggered back and his hand went to his side, but before he could draw a weapon, Jack had him covered with his own automatic and spoke quietly.

"One move and you are a dead man," he said quietly.

"Who are you?" asked the man in a low voice.

"British officers," said Lord Hastings. "And you?"

"Captain Bretog, commander of this vessel," came the reply.

"Very good, captain," said Lord Hastings. "You are our prisoner, and I must ask you to step upon the bridge."

"How did you get here?" asked the German in surprise.

"In a little submarine of our own," said Lord Hastings with a smile. "Come, now, captain."

The captain moved toward the companionway, but just as he was about to go through the door, he turned and struck out at Lord Hastings. The latter dodged the blow and leaped quickly back, at the same time drawing his revolver.

"No more of that," he said sternly. "Now move."

But at that instant a German sailor appeared in sight. Perceiving the British uniforms, he cried out in surprise. An instant more and there came the sound of tramping feet, and half a dozen men tumbled into sight after him.

Lord Hastings put the German commander in front of him, and Jack stepped quickly to his commander's side, their four automatics covering the superior numbers of the enemy.

"One move from any of you and you are all dead men," said Lord Hastings calmly. "We'll shoot you where you stand, and my vessel will blow you to atoms within half a minute." He turned to the German commander.

"Captain," he said, "order these men on deck ahead of you."

The German made a move as though to refuse, but Jack's revolver covered him and he did as commanded. The men, unarmed, filed up to the bridge.

"You next, captain," said Lord Hastings, politely, stepping aside.

The German made a move as though to draw a revolver, and Jack was at his side in an instant.

"I'll relieve you of your weapons," he said quietly.

The German commander was forced to submit while the lad searched him and took his guns. Then, at another command from Lord Hastings, he followed his men on deck.

"Now," said Lord Hastings, "you will instruct your men to lower that small boat and put off. Is this all your crew, sir?"

"Yes," replied the German shortly.

"Good. For their sakes I hope you are telling the truth. For as soon as we are all safe, I intend to sink this vessel. Now order your men over the side."

The German commander did as commanded, and soon the crew of the Teuton vessel were pulling away in the launch.

"Now, captain," said Lord Hastings, "you will accompany me aboard my own ship."

The German stepped into the D-16's launch without a word, and the trio were soon aboard.

"Now," said Lord Hastings, "if you wish, you shall have the pleasure of seeing me sink your vessel; or you may, if you would spare yourself that sight, go below."

"I will go below if you please," said the German.

Lord Hastings nodded his assent and Captain Bretog disappeared below as Lord Hastings turned to Jack.

"You may sink this German submarine immediately, Mr. Templeton," he said quietly.

"Very good, sir," replied Jack.

He saluted, turned on his heel and went below.

CHAPTER X.

IN THE KIEL CANAL.

Five minutes later and the D-16 was once more on her way, while behind her the ruins of a German submarine strewed the sea.

Immediately the D-16 had again submerged, Lord Hastings summoned Jack, Frank and the captured German officer to his quarters. Here, after motioning all to seats, he addressed the German commander.

"Captain," he said quietly, "you are now aboard a British submarine that is about to attempt a passage of the Kiel canal."

"What!" exclaimed the German officer, jumping to his feet. "It is impossible!"

"You are mistaken, sir," replied Lord Hastings calmly. "With your help, I should say that it would be a matter of little moment."

"With my help?" inquired the German officer.

"Exactly. You shall give us your assistance."

"But, sir — —" began the German.

Lord Hastings interrupted him with a wave of his hand.

"Protests will do no good," he said quietly. "I take it that you are familiar with the locations of the mines and other danger points in and guarding the entrance to the canal. Am I right?"

The German officer bowed his head in assent.

"Then," said Lord Hastings, "I fail to see why we should have much difficulty getting through."

"You mean," said the German slowly, "that you expect me to pilot your vessel through the canal?"

Lord Hastings bowed courteously.

"Exactly," he replied.

The German officer drew himself up indignantly.

"That, sir," he said, "is hardly a fair thing to ask of a prisoner."

"Perhaps not, you being the prisoner," replied the commander of the D-16. "Still, you may have heard that 'All's fair in love and war.'"

"And if I refuse?" said the German.

"Well, it's hard to say," replied Lord Hastings quietly. "But I can say this much: We cannot be burdened with any human excess."

"You mean you will kill me?"

"Oh, no; nothing like that. Rather, I should suggest setting you adrift in a small boat."

The German was silent for some moments, musing.

"And I might say," continued Lord Hastings, "that you would be given no water or provisions."

"You might just as well shoot me outright," said the German.

Lord Hastings shrugged his shoulders.

"I couldn't quite do that," he replied.

"Well," said the German officer, "if I must, I must, and that's all there is about it."

"I am glad you are so sensible," said Lord Hastings. "Now, I shall turn the vessel over to you at once; but remember, at the first sign of treachery, there will always be a bullet waiting for you."

The German bowed, but made no reply. Lord Hastings summoned a sailor, and instructed him to put the German officer in charge of the helm, but to keep close watch over him. The sailor and the German commander then left Lord Hastings' quarters.

"Great Scott!" exclaimed Frank when they had gone. "Do you mean to tell me that you would have carried out your threat?"

"Well, hardly," replied his commander with a laugh. "However, as you see, a threat in the proper place often works out advantageously."

"Still," said Jack, "I am not exactly satisfied that he means to play straight with us. He gave in too easily to suit me."

"The same thought struck me," declared Frank.

"Oh, I guess he'll put us through," said Lord Hastings.

"I'm not so sure," from Frank skeptically.

"Well," said Lord Hastings, "we'll watch him carefully, and his first false step will be his last. We can't afford to take chances now. One of us must be near him all the time."

Thus it was arranged and Jack volunteered to take the first watch. Frank elected to take the second and Lord Hastings announced that he would take the third. This watch, it was agreed, would be maintained until they had passed through the canal.

Jack made his way at once to the helm, where he took up his station, while Frank and Lord Hastings turned in. Here the lad sat for four straight hours, not once relaxing his vigilance. Then Frank relieved him.

All went well in this second watch until there was but an hour of it left. Then the German commander turned to Frank.

"I'll have to ask you to rise three fathoms," he said.

"Rise?" said Frank. "What for?"

"Because," was the reply, "the water is very shallow just ahead, and we shall run aground. We are now approaching the entrance to the canal."

Frank looked at his captive long and searchingly. There was still a doubt of the German's honesty of purpose in his mind, and for a moment he was undecided.

"We must rise at once," said the German.

Frank made his decision quickly. "Very well," he said quietly.

He stepped to the signal tube and gave the necessary order. A moment later the rising of the vessel became perceptible, as the water was slowly forced from her tanks.

Frank, not perfectly satisfied, however, stood facing the German officer, his hand on his revolver, determined to use it at the first sign of treachery.

But his uneasiness was without cause. When the submarine had risen the required distance, at a word from the German, her speed was increased and she moved forward again.

"Is there not danger of striking a mine up here?" asked Frank.

"There are a few about," was the reply, "but I can guarantee that we shall not strike one. When the depth of the water permits, we shall go lower again."

With this Frank was forced to be satisfied.

His four hours up, Frank was relieved by Lord Hastings, to whom he related what had occurred.

Lord Hastings listened quietly.

"I'm sure he will try no tricks," he said. "However, I'll keep an eye on him."

"Still," said Frank, "I have a premonition that all is not right."

Lord Hastings laughed, and Frank retired.

Now the Kiel canal is not very long, sixty-one miles of water connecting the North and Baltic seas. It extends across the narrowest portion of Germany close to the boundary between Germany and Denmark, thus making a passage for German vessels from one sea to the other.

Lord Hastings had kept his own reckoning and believed, while he was not familiar with these waters, that he could determine when the Baltic end of the canal had been reached.

And, indeed, it seemed that he was right.

It was just after his watch, when Jack had relieved him and while he lingered in the compartment, that the German turned to Lord Hastings and said:

"You may rise now. You have done what it has been believed impossible for any hostile ship to do. You have passed through the Kiel canal."

At that moment Frank, refreshed by a few hours' sleep, entered.

As Lord Hastings was about to give the signal to rise, Frank stepped forward.

"One moment, sir," he exclaimed. "Something tells me that all is not right. We had best be careful, sir."

The German drew himself up.

"Do you mean to insinuate — —" he began.

Jack silenced him with a word. Then he, too, turned to Lord Hastings.

"I can't explain why, sir," he said, "but I believe Frank is right. Also, you may remember, sir, how he has been right on more than one occasion and that you said hereafter you would place unusual confidence in his premonitions."

"Bosh," said Lord Hastings scornfully. "It is true I did say that, but this time there can be no mistake. I have kept the reckoning myself, and the German is right. By this time we should have reached the Baltic end of the canal."

"But, sir," protested Frank, "could he not have steered us the same distance, but in another direction? Is it not possible that when we come up we may be right in a nest of the enemy's ships, or under the guns of their fortifications?"

"It is possible, yes," replied Lord Hastings, "but you are wrong. You are both letting your imaginations run away with you. No; I am sure the man is up to no trick."

"At least, sir," protested Frank, "do not rise clear to the surface without looking about through the periscope."

"That is good advice, and it shall be heeded," said Lord Hastings. "Mr. Templeton, you may give the command to rise."

Jack saluted and did as commanded, and with the periscope just above the water, the D-16 became stationary. Frank put his eye to the periscope and started back with an exclamation of dismay.

At the same moment the German officer sprang to the signal tube, and, in perfect English, gave the command to rise to the surface.

Jack took in the situation upon the instant and sprang toward the German even as he leaped toward the tube. But he was too late, and before he could countermand the order, the D-16 floated upon the surface of the water.

Jack, in the meantime, was grappling with the German officer, who had drawn a concealed revolver and was attempting to bring it to bear upon Lord Hastings. Frank sprang to his assistance, and Lord Hastings, unmindful of the struggle, and thinking only of the mistake he had made, stepped quickly from the compartment, and opening the conning tower, made his way to the bridge.

And there, he, too, started back in dismay, and no wonder. For what his eyes beheld was this:

Dead ahead rose the sheer walls of a massive fortress, the powerful guns of which swept the narrow canal for miles. And at either side, with the D-16 squarely between them, four battle cruisers rode gently on the waves.

Lord Hastings took one quick look at the flags that floated above the big battle cruisers, then dived hurriedly below.

For the flags that fluttered in the breeze were the flags of Germany!

CHAPTER XI.
AT CLOSE QUARTERS.

Below, Jack and Frank were still struggling with the German officer, but Lord Hastings had no time to lend them a hand. He raised his voice in a shout, and the crew came running at his command.

"Submerge instantly!" he cried.

But already sharp eyes aboard the German cruisers had caught sight of the submarine, and even as she sank suddenly from sight a single gun roared. The aim of this particular gunner was excellent; for the periscope of the D-16 was carried away as clean as a whistle.

Lord Hastings, who had been peering through it from below, was instantly aware of what had happened, and he immediately rushed to the compartment where the searchlight was placed and turned it on. This was now the only eye the submarine had with which to look for danger ahead.

Lord Hastings again raised his voice and a sailor came running to him. The commander of the vessel turned the lookout over to him and rushed to where he had left Frank and Jack.

When Frank had gone to his friend's assistance, he had thought that together they would have little trouble overcoming the German officer. But the latter, in spite of Jack's strength and all that Frank could do, was giving a good account of himself.

Blow after blow he landed upon each of the lads, but none had the power behind it to put them down. Time after time the two lads had closed in on him, only to be shaken off for the German was as slippery as an eel.

But finally Jack succeeded in gaining a strangle hold on the German, and putting forth his greatest strength, bore him to the floor, where both lads piled on top of him, pinioning his arms and legs. It was at this moment that Lord Hastings appeared upon the scene and rushed forward to lend a helping hand.

In falling the German's head had come in violent contact with the floor, and he now lay still.

"Tie him up quickly," commanded Lord Hastings. "We haven't any time to waste on him."

Jack and Frank hastened to obey, and soon the captive was securely bound.

The two lads noticed the signs of anxiety on their commander's face and Frank asked:

"What's the matter, sir?"

"Matter is that we are in a veritable nest of the enemy," replied Lord Hastings. "Also our periscope has been shot away."

"But we can rig up the other in no time," said Jack.

"So we can," said his commander, "but in the meantime they are likely to send a flotilla of submarines below to look for us."

"Then we shall have to hustle," said Frank.

"Hustle is the proper word," agreed Lord Hastings. "Come with me."

He led the way to the foot of the broken periscope, and quickly summoned several members of the crew. With all possible haste the second periscope, carried for just such an emergency, was brought out and run up.

"The only way we can tell whether it is adjusted properly," said Lord Hastings, "is to rise, and that is exceedingly dangerous."

"Well, we shall have to take a chance," said Frank.

"So we shall," was the reply. "You may give the order, Mr. Templeton."

Jack did as commanded, and slowly the submarine began to rise. Lord Hastings stood at the foot of the second periscope, peering intently into it. At last he raised his hand in a sudden signal, and immediately the vessel began to sink again.

"It's all right," said the commander, turning to the lads. "I caught a glimpse of the surface."

"Then we are all fixed again," said Frank thankfully.

"Yes."

"Then," said Jack, "I should say the thing to do is to put as great distance as possible between us and the enemy."

"The only draw back to that," said Lord Hastings, "is that I do not know just where we are and to move in any direction is decidedly dangerous."

"Weren't you able to recognize the surroundings?" asked Frank.

"No; the canal is fortified all along, and all the fortifications look alike to me."

"Well," said Jack, "how about the prisoner? Don't you think he can be made to pilot us out of danger?"

"No," was the reply, "I don't. I am absolutely positive he would refuse, no matter what the result. I am convinced that the only reason he agreed before was because he figured he could put us in the power of his friends. I don't believe he scared worth a cent."

"Nor I," agreed Frank.

"Well, then what is to be done?" asked Jack.

"We shall just have to feel our way along carefully," replied Lord Hastings. "But we must get away from this spot immediately. There is no telling what they may dump over on us. Straight ahead, Mr. Templeton, at seven knots."

"Very good, sir," replied the lad, and repeated the command to the engine room.

Lord Hastings himself took the helm, and Frank again stood watch in the forward compartment. For an hour they proceeded without incident, and then Lord Hastings decided to rise and take a look about.

Accordingly the pumps were set to work, and as the water was forced from the submersion tanks, the D-16 rose toward the surface. Lord Hastings, Frank and Jack ascended to the bridge.

"Well," said the former, "we seem to have given them the slip."

"It looks that way, sir," replied Frank, after a quick glance over the water.

In the distance they could make out the forms of the battle cruisers, but evidently those aboard the German vessels did not perceive the submarine, lying low in the water.

Suddenly as the three stood talking, a figure bounded upon the bridge from below, and before any of the three could raise a hand to stop him, crossed the deck and hurled himself into the sea.

"Great Scott!" cried Frank. "It's the German!"

"Impossible!" exclaimed Jack. "He was too securely bound to free himself."

"But I am positive that is who it was," said Frank.

All rushed to the side of the bridge, and peered intently into the water, waiting for the figure of the man to reappear upon the surface. Perhaps a minute later, they made out his form, quite a distance from the vessel, and swimming toward the distant German vessels with powerful strokes.

"Now I wonder how he managed to get— —" began Jack, and paused suddenly.

For Frank, throwing off his coat, had hurled himself into the water and set out in pursuit of the fugitive.

"Here! Come back here!" called Jack to his friend.

Lord Hastings added his voice to Jack's.

"Come back," he cried. "Let him go."

Frank waved one arm in the air and called back over his shoulder:

"I'll get him. You wait right here for me if I am gone a year!"

Jack turned to Lord Hastings.

"Shall I jump over and bring him back?" he asked.

Lord Hastings shook his head.

"No," he replied. "Let him go. If he can catch the German, all right; but I doubt it. However, when he finds that the chase is hopeless and that he is likely to fall into the hands of the enemy, he will turn back."

"I'm not so sure about that," said Jack. "Frank is rather hot headed at times, you know, and he is likely to chase him clear aboard a German warship."

"I give him credit for more sense than that," said Lord Hastings.

"So do I," said Jack, "at times. At other times he loses his head altogether."

"Well, the best thing we can do is to wait and see what happens," said Lord Hastings. "The only thing that worries me is that the German may prove more than a match for him should he overtake him."

"I'll leave it to Frank to get himself out of any trouble like that," said Jack. "The only thing that I am afraid of is his hot-headedness."

In the meantime, exert himself as he would, Frank realized that he was not lessening the distance between himself and the fugitive; but the lad was not one to give up the chase so easily. He gritted his teeth and muttered to himself:

"I'll get him if I have to chase him all around the world."

After a time Frank's hopes arose, for a quick look ahead showed him that he had gained a trifle. This encouraging sign lent strength to his arms. He struck out more vigorously than before, as he realized that it was only a question of time until he overtook his quarry.

But what the lad did not know was that at that very instant the lookout on the nearest German warship had caught sight of the two swimmers. A shouted command aboard the German vessel, and a launch put off over the side and dashed rapidly toward the German officer in the water.

This Frank did not see, and so swam on in ignorance of the danger that threatened. Raising his eyes, a couple of minutes later he saw the German officer as he was picked up by the boat, and for the first time realized that he was in a ticklish situation.

"Great Scott!" he muttered to himself. "Why didn't I keep my eyes open? I hope they are satisfied with saving him and let me alone."

He turned quickly, and made for the D-16 as fast as he could swim.

But his hopes were to prove fruitless, as a quick glance over his shoulder told him. In the launch he perceived the German commander gesticulating violently and pointing in his direction.

"I guess it's up to me to hustle," he told himself.

Now the German launch started after him, gaining at every stroke the lad made.

Lord Hastings and Jack perceived the turn of affairs, and Jack cried out:

"Get the launch over quick and man it. Unless we can lick these fellows, Frank is a goner."

The crew acted with promptness, and in a twinkling the launch of the D-16 also was racing toward the swimming lad.

CHAPTER XII.
CAPTURED.

Frank, literally the bone of contention between the two forces in the launches, swam as swiftly as possible in the direction of safety; but the furtive glances he cast over his shoulder showed him that the Germans were nearer than his friends, and that in spite of the fact that he was swimming toward the latter, the former would come up with him first.

The men in both boats were now on their feet, and their revolvers spoke across the water. As yet, however, they were too far away to make accurate shooting possible, and no one was even touched.

But soon the German boat drew so close to Frank, that the men in the D-16's launch were afraid to fire at the Germans for fear a chance shot might hit the lad. The Germans, however, were not thus handicapped, and continued pouring lead in the direction of Lord Hastings and his men.

As the German boat came alongside Frank, a man reached out to grab him. Frank took a long breath and dived, the fingers of his foe just touching his shoulder.

When he came to the surface for a fresh breath, the German boat was several yards away and Frank breathed easier.

"If I can keep that up," he told himself, "I may get away yet."

Again the boat drew near and again Frank dived.

The German officer in command had had enough of this game of hide and seek, however, and he immediately ordered two of his men overboard after the lad.

Frank, of course, knew nothing of this move and when he came to the surface once more, he was surprised to find rough hands laid upon him from both sides. In vain did he strike out with both feet and hands. Struggle as he would he could not shake off his foes; and all three sank together.

The German boat came closer, and the sailors leaned over the side, ready to pull in the struggling trio when they came to the surface again.

Sputtering and gasping for breath, the three heads finally showed above the water. There was not much fight left in any of them, and therefore Frank was drawn over the side without much trouble. Then the German officer ordered the launch brought about, and put off for the German cruiser at full speed.

As they fled, a running battle with the men in the D-16's launch ensued. One German toppled over into the water, but the boat was not stopped to pick him up. One British sailor was struck in the arm by a German bullet; but outside of these two no one was wounded.

The German launch had the heels of the D-16's small boat, and soon outdistanced her. Convinced at last that pursuit was useless, Lord Hastings ordered that the chase be abandoned. The launch was brought about and headed slowly back toward the submarine.

"Poor Frank," said Jack. "I always knew his rashness would get him in trouble some day. I am afraid his days of fighting are over."

"While there is life there is hope," said Lord Hastings calmly. "Perhaps we may be able to figure out some means of rescue."

"A great chance," said Jack sarcastically. "Right in the heart of the enemy's country? I don't think so. What do you suppose they will do with him?"

"Hold him as a prisoner of war."

"Then there is no danger of his being shot?"

"I should say not."

"Well, that's not so bad. Still, it is pretty tough for him to be cooped up for the next few years."

Aboard the D-16 once more, all went below immediately and Lord Hastings gave the command to submerge.

"They know we are here now," he said, "and they'll be after us. Therefore we had better get down. We'll stay around for a while and see if we cannot be of some help to Frank. We may be able to maneuver so as to avoid detection."

"When it comes to that," said Jack, "we might as well be here as any place else. I should say that there is considerable work we could do hereabouts, and if we can avoid the enemy we can make it pretty warm for them."

"You are right," replied Lord Hastings, "but we shall have to be very careful, for, knowing we are here, they will undoubtedly have every ship in these waters looking for us."

"Well," said Jack, "why should we wait for them to act? Why can't we strike the first blow?"

Lord Hastings looked at him quizzically.

"Just what do you mean by that?" he asked.

"Why," said Jack, "torpedo one of them right now."

"I am afraid you are a little hot headed yourself," said his commander with a faint smile. "I should say that that is just what they expect us to do, and for that reason I am opposed to such action. Never do the expected, is my motto. It is the unexpected that counts."

"Perhaps you are right," agreed Jack; "still I would like to get at a few of them."

"Don't fret," said Lord Hastings, "you shall have your chance."

Meanwhile, what of Frank?

Immediately the launch had returned to the German cruiser, the lad was hurried over the side and taken to the commander's cabin. The latter received him courteously and motioned him to a seat.

"And how, if I may ask," he inquired, "do you happen to be in the middle of the Kiel canal?"

Frank smiled slightly.

"I came in a submarine," he replied.

"So I have perceived," said the commander.

"But I was unaware England had established a submarine base anywhere near German territory."

"Neither has she, to my knowledge," said Frank.

"Then how did you get here? Surely you must have a base."

"Our base," said Frank, "was London."

"What?" exclaimed the German, jumping to his feet. "You sit here and tell me a thing like that? Surely you can't think I don't know that a submarine cannot operate that distance from her base."

"Nevertheless, it is true," replied Frank quietly.

"But your air supply, your torpedoes, your provisions," exclaimed the German commander.

"Those we carry with us," said Frank.

"Then," said the German sarcastically, "yours must be a very remarkable submarine."

"So it is," replied Frank.

"Well, it will be impossible for her to get away," said the German. "We have her bottled up, and all we need do is wait until she comes to the surface to replenish her air tanks; then we can sink her."

"You'll have a long wait," said Frank. "She doesn't have to come up for that purpose."

"What do you mean by that?"

"Just what I say. The submarine to which I am attached carries no air tanks except those to be used in case of an emergency."

"No air tanks! Then how do you get air?"

"Well," said Frank, "I can't see that it will do any harm to tell you. We extract air from the water."

The German commander leaned back in his chair and looked at the lad in amazement.

"Extract air from the water, eh?" he said slowly. "Do you mean to tell me that England has solved that problem?"

"She has, sir," replied Frank quietly.

The German was silent for a long time before he said: "Then I must say that Germany has a hard job on her hands."

Frank was silent and the captain continued:

"And how many such vessels have you in operation?"

Frank hesitated.

"Well, only a few right now," he said at last. "But many more are in the process of construction."

"And are you familiar with the operations of such a vessel, and of the method used?"

"To a certain extent, yes."

"But I do not suppose you could be prevailed upon to divulge the secret?"

"I could not," replied Frank quietly.

"Good! I thought not. Well, it's too bad that we were not the first to discover the secret; but you will find that we do not whine, nor will we seek to obtain the secret by unfair means."

"I am sure of it, sir," replied Frank.

"Now," said the German commander, "I must decide what I am going to do with you. I suppose that you know you will be held until the end of the war?"

Frank nodded as he replied: "I should suppose so."

"I shall have you sent ashore in the morning and turned over to the military authorities. The chances are that you will be taken to Berlin. Of that I am not sure, however."

"One place will do as well as another, I suppose."

"I'm glad you are cheerful about it," laughed the captain, "and as mess hour is approaching I shall be glad to have you dine with me."

"I shall be pleased to do so, sir."

"By the way," said the German, "what is the speed of this remarkable submarine of yours?"

"I wouldn't like to say," replied Frank, "but I can say that it is fully as great as that of your fastest battleship."

The German puckered his lips in a long expressive whistle.

"Well," he said, "it's too bad for us. Now, if you care to wash up I shall have you shown to your temporary quarters."

It was a pleasant meal to which the lad sat down that evening, and he enjoyed himself immensely. He found the German officers a likeable lot and was treated more as a guest than as a prisoner.

It was while at table that he learned that German submarines had been sent down in search of the British vessel, and that each battleship was being guarded by an under-the-sea fighter so that no surprise attack by the D-16 might be made.

At a late hour the lad retired and slept the sleep of the exhausted.

He was up bright and early the following morning, and after breakfast took his place in the ship's launch, which immediately headed toward the shore. The captain bade him a pleasant good-bye, and added:

"If I get to Berlin I shall look you up."

"I'm not there yet," said Frank, but in his heart he was pretty sure that it was only a question of hours until he would be.

CHAPTER XIII.
A SUBMARINE RAID.

Creeping stealthily forward beneath the water, the D-16 was advancing to the attack. Lord Hastings stood at the periscope and Jack was at his elbow. The vessel was prepared for action, and the crew stood at attention.

Lord Hastings touched Jack on the shoulder.

"Tell the watch to keep a sharp lookout for submarines," he said. "The chances are that they have been thrown out in front of the battleships."

Jack departed and gave the necessary order, after which he returned to his position.

It was just after dusk on the evening following the day on which Frank had been captured. All day and all during the previous night the D-16 had kept near the bottom, maneuvering first this way and then that, and not once had they caught sight of an enemy's submarine, nor had they risen to the surface for a look about.

But now Lord Hastings had decided upon action. He had idled long enough. Therefore, after preparing for action, the D-16 had risen sufficiently to give her periscope free play, and the commander now gazed over the water.

"German battleship ahead," he called to Jack. "Slow to five knots."

The speed of the submarine slackened.

"Take the lookout yourself, Mr. Templeton," was the next command.

Jack did as commanded, and peered intently ahead. In the dark murky water he could see but a few feet, for it had not been deemed advisable to turn on the searchlight and thus make a target for the enemy's submarines.

However, the D-16 was progressing at a snail's pace and could be halted upon the instant. Therefore, there was not much danger of encountering any obstacle, providing the man on lookout attended to his duties properly.

Suddenly a dark object loomed up ahead. Quick as a flash Jack signalled the engine room and the D-16 came to an abrupt stop. Jack reported to Lord Hastings.

"Dark object right ahead that looks like a submarine submerged," he said calmly.

"Give the order to back away a hundred yards, then fire a torpedo into her," was Lord Hastings' command.

Slowly the D-16 backed away from the dark object ahead, and an instant later a sharp "click" gave evidence that a torpedo had been launched. Immediately Jack flashed on the searchlight.

While his eyes could not follow the flight of the torpedo, the huge and powerful searchlight showed him the result. Struck squarely amidships the German submarine, for such the object ahead proved to be, seemed to split wide open. The water poured in in a dense volume, and suddenly the enemy sank.

Jack shuddered.

"Must be a terrible death," he muttered to himself. "However, if we had not sunk her she would probably have sunk us."

Once more he reported to Lord Hastings.

"Way clear now, sir," he said.

"Good," was the reply. "Make your speed five knots and continue your course."

Perhaps ten minutes more and then Lord Hastings gave the command to heave to. For, through the periscope, less than a quarter of a mile away, he could make out the form of a giant German battle cruiser, a trifle to starboard.

The electric signal board flashed its message of death:

"No. 5 torpedo!"

"Ready!"

"Fire!"

"Click!"

Just this little sound and then Lord Hastings gave the command to rise, for he wished to witness the effect of the torpedo on the German cruiser.

The D-16 rose swiftly, but not as swiftly as the torpedo had sped on its way. For when the submarine reached the surface the torpedo had already done its work, and the German cruiser was helpless. Men were jumping into the sea on all sides and swimming away.

Jack was struck with a sudden idea. He turned to Lord Hastings.

"If we could pick up one of those fellows," he said, pointing, "perhaps we could find out what has happened to Frank."

"Good," replied Lord Hastings, "it shall be done."

Upon his command the submarine forged ahead slowly directly toward the doomed German cruiser. Heads of men swimming began to bob up and down on both sides. Jack, leaning over the side, which was almost level with the water, suddenly stretched forth a hand and dragged a German petty officer aboard.

Frightened almost out of his wits, for he had not perceived the dark outline of the submarine, the German struggled fiercely; but he was no match for Jack, who soon subdued him.

The man was dragged below, and upon Jack's request, the submarine was again submerged.

When the prisoner learned that he was aboard the British submarine he braced up, and when he found that he was not to be harmed, he proved willing to talk.

"Where is the English prisoner whom you captured yesterday?" Lord Hastings asked him.

"He has been sent ashore," was the reply. "He was to have been taken to Berlin today, to be held as a prisoner of war; but I understand that for some reason it was put off till tomorrow."

"I see," said Lord Hastings, and as he did not wish to put the prisoner on his guard, he talked for some minutes of other matters.

"By the way," he said finally, "how is our friend guarded? Is he locked in a cell, or what?"

"Yes," was the reply. "He refused to give his parole, so naturally he had to be confined. However, he is perfectly comfortable and is being well cared for."

"So he is locked up in the fort," said Lord Hastings. "Then there is no chance of his being so foolish as to attempt to escape."

"It certainly would be foolish," said the prisoner, "although once outside the cell, he might lose himself for a while; but of course there would be no chance of his getting out of the country. You see, we are perfectly safe here, or were until you came along, so it is unnecessary to keep such a close watch."

"And where is the fort where he is confined?" asked Lord Hastings.

"Only a short distance from the edge of the canal. It is called Fort Kaiserin."

"Well," said Lord Hastings as he turned away, having learned all that he desired to know, "I guess we had better get away from this spot or one of your submarines is liable to find us. Mr. Templeton, you may escort the prisoner to your own quarters and place a sailor on guard."

Jack led the prisoner to his own cabin and, after stationing a sailor at the door, returned to Lord Hastings.

"What have you on your mind, sir?" he asked.

"What do you mean?" asked his commander.

"Why," said Jack, "I know you were not asking all those questions for nothing."

"That is true," was the reply. "I was thinking that by donning German uniforms and going ashore, we might possibly rescue Frank."

"I had thought of that myself, sir; and I believe it might be done."

"So do I."

"Then shall we make the attempt, sir?"

"Yes," replied Lord Hastings, "we shall."

"Good. When?"

"At once. We have no time to lose."

"But the submarine. How shall we know where to find her?"

"I'll fix that. Send Brennan to me."

Jack departed and returned a moment later with Brennan, the chief engineer.

"Brennan," said Lord Hastings, "Mr. Templeton and I are going to take the launch and go ashore. As soon as we have gone I want you to submerge just to the edge of the periscope and remain there until you see us returning. Then rise immediately to take us aboard, for we may come in a hurry."

"But if an enemy should approach in the meantime, sir?" asked Brennan.

"In that case you will, of course, submerge at once, and then, making a detour, return to approximately the same spot. It may be necessary to take chances, but you will have to do that."

"Very good, sir," said Brennan, saluting.

Lord Hastings turned to Jack.

"We'll go to the surface now," he said. "We may as well start at once."

Five minutes later, in the little launch, they were skimming over the water toward the shore, which they could just see in the darkness. They felt sure that they had quitted the submarine unobserved.

As soon as they were over the side, Brennan, in accordance with instructions, had immediately submerged.

Before leaving they had both attired themselves in German uniforms, and felt comparatively safe.

The run to shore took perhaps fifteen minutes.

When they at last set foot on land their first thought was for a hiding place for the launch. Several trees overhanging the canal at the point where they had landed afforded a slight shelter and into their shadow the launch was pulled.

"It's the best we can do, and I guess she won't be seen," said Jack.

"At any rate we'll have to take a chance," replied Lord Hastings. "Now let's go."

They turned their faces westward, where, in the distance, they could make out the outlines of the German fortifications.

"How are we going to know which is Fort Kaiserin?" asked Jack.

"We'll have to ask," was the reply.

"Won't that give us away?"

"I don't think so. We can say we just came here."

This plan was followed and a soldier directed them to the fort. They were just about to enter it and trust to luck, when their attention was attracted by the sound of a scuffle a short distance down the street.

"Let's see what it is about," said Jack. "It may help us in some way."

Lord Hastings nodded his assent, and they dashed toward a struggling knot of men only a few yards away.

CHAPTER XIV.
THE ESCAPE.

When Frank reached shore after being taken from the German cruiser, he was received courteously by the officer in command of Fort Kaiserin—one of the German fortifications along the Kiel canal. The latter questioned him at length regarding the D-16, and the lad gave what information he believed could be of no value to the enemy.

At first it was announced that the lad would be taken to Berlin that day, but later as the reader has already learned this was deferred till the next.

"If you will give me your parole," said the German commander, "I shall be glad to allow you the freedom of the fort."

"I appreciate your kindness," replied Frank, "and I am sorry that I do not feel myself at liberty to accept."

The officer shrugged his shoulders.

"There is little danger of your getting away," he said. "However, I find it my duty, in view of your refusal, to order you confined."

Frank bowed but said nothing.

Half an hour later he was conducted to a cell at the end of the fort nearest the outer wall. Here he sat all day, being well treated and well fed, but allowed no liberty.

"By George!" said Frank to himself right after noon, "I have a notion to try to get out of here. I don't know whether I can get away or not, but I believe I shall take a chance at it. I don't want to be cooped up in Berlin for the next few years if I can help it."

Accordingly he mapped out a plan, which he decided to put into execution when the jailer brought his evening meal.

The afternoon passed slowly, but at length the time to act came.

A key grated in the cell door and the jailer entered, carrying a tray of food.

"How is the weather outside?" asked Frank.

The jailer was a jovial sort.

"Fine," he replied. "Too bad you cannot be out to enjoy it."

"It is too bad," Frank agreed. "Well, what do I get for supper?" and he bent over as though to examine the tray.

"Soup — —" began the jailer, but he said no more.

Straightening up suddenly, Frank caught the man by the throat with a vise-like grip, while he clapped his other hand over his mouth, stifling an outcry. Then, suddenly, he drew back his right fist, and before the German could free himself, struck him full on the point of the jaw.

The German toppled over like a log.

Frank picked him up gently and laid him on the bed, where he gagged him with his handkerchief.

"Now to get out," he said.

He approached the door and peered about. There was no one in sight. He picked up the jailer's keys and, stepping into the corridor, closed the door behind him and locked it.

"Now if I can just avoid detection till I get out of here," he told himself.

Quietly he walked along the corridor, to where he knew the door to be. In a room just beyond he heard voices. He approached carefully and peered in.

In a far corner, half a dozen German soldiers were busily engaged with a pack of cards. They were so engrossed in their game that they paid no attention to Frank as he stepped quietly into the room, walked boldly across it and disappeared through the door on the opposite side.

Outside Frank drew a long breath.

"So far so good," he muttered.

Getting into the open was now a simple matter. Frank knew full well that a careful watch was not being kept, so now he walked boldly on.

Turning eastward and feeling that he was free at last, he broke into a quick trot.

This almost proved his undoing, for suddenly a voice out of the darkness challenged him.

"Who goes there?"

"Friend," replied Frank.

The challenger approached. One glance at his British naval uniform was enough. The man attempted to bring his gun to bear, but Frank was too quick for him. Jumping suddenly forward, he knocked up the weapon, and then, with two terrific punches, laid the man low.

But the sound of this scuffle had attracted half a dozen other figures and now Frank found himself surrounded.

"They will have to fight to take me back there," he said through clenched teeth, and not waiting for his foes to come to the attack, he plunged into the midst of them.

When Jack and Lord Hastings advanced toward the struggling knot of men they had no idea what was going on; but Frank, over the shoulders of his foes, saw them.

"Jack! Lord Hastings!" he cried.

His two friends were taken aback, but Jack was the first to recover himself.

"It's Frank!" he cried, and dashed forward.

Lord Hastings was not a moment behind him, and these reinforcements, seeming to be two German officers, disconcerted Frank's adversaries, who drew off.

But the sound of Jack's voice speaking in English convinced them that something was wrong, and they sprang forward again.

"Crack!"

With a single movement Jack had drawn his revolver and fired.

One man fell.

"Crack! Crack! Crack! Crack!"

The firing became general, but the Germans were taken at a disadvantage as their opponents had been the first to draw.

Three Germans only now remained on their feet, and as Lord Hastings, Jack and Frank advanced upon them they turned and fled.

"Quick!" cried Lord Hastings. "Follow me! We'll have the whole garrison upon us in a moment!"

He turned and dashed back along the dark road, Frank and Jack following.

From behind came the sounds of a terrible commotion. The garrison was aroused, and the fugitives realized that speed was the only thing that would save their lives.

Without a word they sped along as fast as their legs would carry them. In the darkness Lord Hastings would have passed the spot where they had hidden the launch had not Jack's keen eyes recognized it as he flashed by.

"Wait!" he called, stopping so suddenly that Frank, who was directly behind him, bumped him and almost knocked him off his feet.

Lord Hastings also stopped.

"What's the matter?" he demanded.

"You have gone too far," cried Jack. "Here!"

He stepped in under the trees and laid a hand upon the launch. Frank and Lord Hastings lent a helping hand, and soon the little boat was floating upon the water.

"Quick! In with you!" cried Jack, as he fairly pushed his two companions into the boat.

Then he gave it a hard shove and scrambled in himself.

At that moment, from behind, came the sound of running footsteps and a hoarse voice of command:

"Fire!"

There was a deafening crash and a hail of bullets sped over the little boat, for at the command fire Jack had cried out:

"Down!"

All three lay flat in the bottom of the boat, Jack, with one hand behind him, doing the steering from that position.

A second and a third hail of bullets from behind passed without harming them, and then no more came.

The three sat up in the boat.

"Pretty close, if you ask me," said Jack.

"I should say so," replied Frank. "We---- Hello!"

"Now what's the matter?" demanded Lord Hastings.

"Listen!" whispered Frank.

All three listened intently.

From astern came a choking "Chug chug."

"We are followed!" exclaimed Frank. "We shall have to hurry. Is this as fast as this thing can move?"

Jack was tinkering with the motor.

"I guess it is," he said at last. "However, we have quite a start, and with luck should be able to reach our vessel before they can overtake us."

As swiftly as she could go the launch made for the spot where the submarine, still submerged, awaited them.

Brennan, whom Lord Hastings had left in command, was fully alive to his responsibility. Steadfastly he remained at his post, peering intently through the periscope. For hours he had been there, and now his patience was rewarded.

In the distance he could make out a small boat dashing madly toward him. Quickly he gave the signal to rise, and when the submarine again floated upon the surface of the water, he ascended to the bridge.

As the boat drew nearer he recognized its occupants; and then, for the first time, he realized that they were followed. Prompt action would be required when they were on board and he knew it.

With a hoarse bellow he called the crew to their places, and advanced to the side of the vessel to lend a hand to the officers when they should arrive.

At last they reached the side, under a volley from the pursuing German launch. Lord Hastings clambered aboard and Frank and Jack followed in rapid succession. As they set foot on deck the latter shouted:

"Below! Quick!"

All made a mad dash and in a moment the entrance through the conning tower was hermetically sealed behind them.

"Submerge!" cried Lord Hastings; and as the D-16 once more sank from view, her commander wiped the beads of perspiration from his forehead with his sleeve.

"Whew!" he exclaimed. "Pretty close! Pretty close! But we are all safe, and that's enough!"

"Right, sir," said Jack. "And enough's a plenty!"

CHAPTER XV.
INTO THE BALTIC.

Lord Hastings called Frank and Jack into consultation to decide upon what should be done.

"We are likely to have all the German submarines in these parts on our trail," he said, "and while we might hope to dispose of some of them, we can hardly hope to beat them all. My advice is that we get out of the Kiel canal at the earliest possible moment."

"I agree with you, sir," said Jack.

"And I, too, sir," declared Frank.

"Good," from Lord Hastings. "Then we shall do so. As long as we are headed for the Baltic, we may as well go in that direction."

So it came about that the British submarine, D-16, plunging swiftly on, struck out boldly for Russian waters.

From the prisoner Lord Hastings was able to get his bearings, and this fact, together with his charts, permitted him to lay a course that would, he believed, bring the submarine into the Baltic Sea in safety.

"Don't you think it would be advisable," asked Frank, "to attempt to sink a couple or more Germans?"

"I hardly think so," was his commander's reply. "We already have done considerable damage and the next venture might not have the same success. No, I believe that we had best be content with what we have done, and get away now."

Jack agreed with Lord Hastings, and Frank, finding that the sentiment was against him, was convinced that he was wrong, and said so.

As the submarine made her way along, Lord Hastings decided that, as they had been so long without news of what was going on at other points in the great war zone, it would be advisable to question their prisoner along this line.

"We'll have him up and learn what's what," he told the two lads.

Accordingly Frank went to fetch him, and a few minutes later all were comfortably seated in the commander's cabin.

Lord Hastings informed the prisoner what they desired of him, and the latter was nothing loath to enlighten them.

"Possibly the matter of greatest moment at this time," said the prisoner with some show of pride, "is the German blockade of Great Britain and the coast of Northern France."

Lord Hastings was on his feet in an instant.

"Blockade of Great Britain!" he ejaculated. "Why, it's impossible. The German fleet itself is bottled up by our ships. How, then, can they blockade England?"

The German smiled.

"It is a blockade, nevertheless," he replied, "if it is only maintained by submarines. No ships of war, nor merchant ships flying the flags of any of our enemies are immune. The blockade went into effect yesterday, and already two merchantmen have been sent to the bottom."

"And their crews?" asked Lord Hastings.

Again the German smiled.

"Who knows?" he replied with a shrug of his shoulders.

"Do you mean to say that they were left to their fate?"

"What else could be done?" asked the prisoner. "The submarines could not provide for them."

"But such action is against all the rules of civilized warfare," exclaimed His Lordship.

"Perhaps so," was the reply. "But as England has not hesitated to take whatever steps she considered necessary, neither will Germany, in the future."

"But the vessels of neutral nations," said Lord Hastings, "are they not in danger because of this blockade?"

"They are—yes," was the reply, "and for this reason: Several British ships already have made their escape by hoisting the Red, White and Blue. However, Germany has defined a well established line of passage for neutral ships, and any found outside of these channels are subject to the same fate as ships of England and France."

"But great Scott, man," exclaimed Lord Hastings, "the sinking of an American ship would more than likely bring the United States into the war against Germany. Surely, you do not desire that."

The German shrugged his shoulders.

"If it cannot be helped," he said quietly, "we are ready to engage the United States also."

"But surely," cried Frank, "you do not believe you can whip the whole world."

"Perhaps not," was the reply, "but neither do we believe the whole world can whip us."

Frank threw up his hands with a gesture of dismay.

"You Germans are about the limit," he said. "It seems to me that you already have bitten off a bigger portion than you can chew, and here you are trying to bring the rest of the civilized world against you."

"We might just as well be whipped by the whole world as a portion of it," said the prisoner.

"And that is my idea of what the Kaiser himself believes," said Jack, who up to this time had taken no part in the conversation. "My opinion is that the German emperor, realizing already that he is fighting a losing fight, is seeking to embroil the whole world."

"But we are not fighting a losing fight," protested the prisoner.

This time it was Lord Hastings who shrugged his shoulders.

"That's a matter of sentiment, of course," he said. "But we didn't call you here to argue with you. What other events of importance are taking place?"

87

"Well," said the prisoner, "in the eastern theater of war we have been successful. Field Marshal Von Hindenburg has defeated the Czar's troops with terrible losses, practically annihilating an entire army corps. Also in the Carpathians and in Northern Poland the Russians have been forced back. In the western war area, reports are conflicting. French and British reports claim some slight successes and the German reports tell of material advances. Of course, we believe the German report to be truthful, while you probably will put more faith in the others.

"But the news that will be the most pleasing to you is the fact that the combined French and British fleets are even now attempting to force a passage of the Dardanelles. Even German reports show that they have met with some success. The first lines of defenses have been shattered, the forts being dismantled and razed. The allied fleets have penetrated twelve miles into the straits."

"By George, that is good news," exclaimed Jack.

"You bet," agreed Frank.

Even Lord Hastings lost his habitual calm and smiled.

"The attempt to force the passage of the Dardanelles," continued the prisoner, "is being led by the monster dreadnought Queen Elizabeth, and it is due to the heavy caliber of her guns that so much success has been attained."

"She is a powerful ship," said Lord Hastings quietly.

"She must be," replied the prisoner. "The others of the fleet follow in her wake, and when she has practically put a fort out of commission they come up and finish the work. She fires her terrible projectiles, and with accuracy, too, a distance of almost twenty miles."

"Twenty miles!" exclaimed Frank.

"Exactly," replied Lord Hastings. "The Queen Elizabeth is probably the most powerful ship of war afloat today."

"Of course," continued the prisoner, "reports received through German sources would indicate that the damage being inflicted by the allied fleet is insignificant. However, reports from other sources lead us to believe that the damage may be greater than even England claims."

"In other words," said Lord Hastings, "it would seem that the forcing of the Dardanelles is only a question of weeks."

"Or even of days," agreed the German.

"Which will clear the road to Constantinople for the Allies."

"Exactly; and Constantinople, according to an agreement between England, France and Russia, is to be turned over to the Czar as a war prize, in case Germany is defeated," said the prisoner.

"Quite a piece of diplomacy," said Lord Hastings. "It will bind the nations of the Triple Entente closer together."

"There is no doubt about that," replied the prisoner. "But that is about all the news I can tell you."

"We are grateful for what you have told us," replied Lord Hastings, "and hope we have not bored you."

"You have not," said the German simply. "But I would like to ask what you intend to do with me?"

Lord Hastings hesitated.

"Well," he said at length, "it is probably plain to you that we cannot afford to be burdened with prisoners. For that reason, if given an opportunity, I had intended to set you adrift in one of the small boats when we were able to come to the surface and are close enough to shore for you to reach if safely."

"You are kind captors, sir," said the German with a bow. "Until such a time, then, I shall return to the quarters you have assigned me. Also, I give my word that I shall make no attempt to escape, nor to interfere with your plans."

"Your parole is accepted, sir," replied Lord Hastings. "The freedom of the ship is yours."

The German bowed low and left the room.

"Do you not fear to trust him?" asked Jack. "Remember the trouble we had with the other officer."

"I am not afraid to trust this one," replied his commander.

"Nor I," agreed Frank. "He is as different from the other as day from night."

Lord Hastings rose and glanced at his watch.

"If I have calculated correctly," he said, "we should by now be beyond the confines of the Kiel canal."

"But," said Frank, "there are still German war vessels and mines in the bays at this end of the Baltic."

"True," replied his commander, "but once out of the canal we will be safe enough, for we can submerge to a greater depth and continue under water until we are safe."

He gave the command to bring the submarine to the surface, and when it floated upon the water, made his way to the bridge. The lads followed him.

"As I thought," said the commander, looking about. "We have reached the Baltic — not the Baltic proper, perhaps, but still Baltic waters."

It was true. Behind could be seen the narrow entrance to the Kiel canal, and ahead the broader expanse of the western arm of the Baltic Sea. There was not a vessel of any kind in sight.

"Well," said Jack. "Looks like we were safe enough here."

"Looks that way," agreed Frank, "but you never can tell, you know."

CHAPTER XVI.
IN TROUBLE AGAIN.

"What's that?" asked Frank, as he gazed across the water.

"Smoke," replied Jack. "It's plain enough."

"I know that," replied the former, "but what I meant is, do you suppose it is a battleship?"

"Looks like it might be," replied Jack briefly.

"Russian or German?" asked Frank.

"Can't tell," said Lord Hastings, who had been peering at the cloud of smoke through his glass. "I can make out that it is a battleship, but that's all. However, we shall know soon enough."

Slowly the cloud of smoke came nearer and nearer, until at last the dim outline of a large battle cruiser of the second class was plainly visible to the naked eye. But still those aboard the D-16 were unable to make out her nationality, for she flew no flag.

"We'd better get ready to dive in case she proves to be a German," said Lord Hastings.

"Right you are, sir," replied Jack, and turning, went below.

Frank and Lord Hastings remained upon the bridge.

Now, of a sudden, there came a faint "boom" across the water.

"Can she have sighted us, sir?" asked Frank anxiously. "Had we not better dive at once?"

"No, I don't think she has sighted us," replied Lord Hastings.

"Then what is she shooting at?"

"You've got me. But that is what we shall have to find out."

Lord Hastings went below, where he ordered the course of the D-16 altered slightly, so as to bring her closer to the far side of the distant cruiser. Then he returned on deck.

Time after time the boom of the big guns could be heard, and those aboard the D-16 were at a loss to make out what the cruiser was firing at. Not another speck was visible on the broad expanse of the Baltic Sea.

"There must be something wrong," said Lord Hastings. "But I can't imagine what— —Hello, she's hoisting her flag."

"Can you make it out, sir?" asked Frank.

Lord Hastings looked long and carefully through his glass.

"Russian," he said at last.

"Good," exclaimed Frank. "We are among friends at any rate."

"I wouldn't be too sure," said his commander. "It may be a German ship that has hoisted the Russian flag for a purpose."

"Well, we'll soon see now," said Frank.

Now the submarine had approached so close that Lord Hastings deemed it advisable to submerge, so that the vessel might not be seen. This was done, and standing at the bottom of the periscope below, the commander of the D-16 took in the scene about him.

Occasional clouds of smoke issued from the cruiser, indicating that her guns were still in action, but for the life of him Lord Hastings could not make out the object of her shots. Also, the cruiser was maneuvering in a strange way, and Lord Hastings could not account for this either.

He stepped aside and Jack took a look through the periscope. Peering long and carefully, he stepped back suddenly with a cry.

"What's the matter?" asked Lord Hastings.

"I've made out the cause of the trouble, sir," said Jack.

"What is it?" demanded his commander.

"Why, sir," replied the lad, "the cruiser is being followed by a submarine— I can just make out her periscope in the distance. That's what the cruiser is firing at. And her strange maneuvering is caused by the fact that she is trying to escape torpedoes. So far she must have been successful."

"In that event," said Lord Hastings, "it is up to us to lend the cruiser a hand. Signal full speed, Mr. Templeton."

Jack obeyed, and the swift British submarine dashed madly through the water.

Suddenly Jack, who was at the periscope, perceived a puff of smoke issue from the forward turret of the cruiser, and a moment later a shell plowed up the water near the D-16.

"We'll have to submerge at once, sir," he said. "The cruiser has sighted us and takes us for an enemy. One of those shells may hit us."

"All right," said Lord Hastings. "First let me have a look."

He stepped to the periscope, which Jack relinquished to him, and peered ahead. Beyond the cruiser he could make out the periscope of another submarine. Calculating the distance. Lord Hastings gave the order to submerge four fathoms.

Then the D-16 dashed in the direction of the submarine that was seeking to destroy the Russian.

Running at 30 knots, the D-16 soon came upon its prey. A dim bulk suddenly loomed up ahead, some distance higher in the water.

"It's the enemy," said Frank, after a careful scrutiny.

"All right," said Lord Hastings. "Give her a shot before she discovers our presence. We can't miss at this distance."

Through the heavy glass in the bow of the submarine Frank watched the effect of the shot. The German submarine staggered suddenly in her stride, then, without a sound, disappeared from sight.

Frank returned to Lord Hastings' side.

"She's gone, sir," he said quietly.

Lord Hastings turned to Jack.

"We'll go to the surface at once," he said.

Hardly had the D-16 bobbed up from beneath the water, when there was a loud boom from the Russian ship now but a short distance away, and a shell screamed overhead.

"Run up the British flag, quick, Mr. Templeton," ordered Lord Hastings.

A moment later the Union Jack fluttered aloft.

Came another shot from the Russian, and a second shell screamed near.

"The fools," cried Lord Hastings angrily. "What do they mean by that?"

"They think we are trying a ruse to get near them, I suppose," replied Frank. "They are unable to tell we are not the same submarine that followed them."

"True," said his commander, "I hadn't thought of that. But how are we to let them know who we are?"

"Well, my idea would be to run up a flag of truce," said Frank. "Then we can explain."

"Good," exclaimed Lord Hastings. "Run up a flag of truce at once."

It was the work of but a few seconds to raise a white flag, and when it had straightened out before the brisk breeze, there was no further shot from the Russian cruiser.

Soon a boat put over the cruiser's side, and manned by a well armed crew, came toward the D-16. Within hailing distance an officer arose and cried out something in a tongue unintelligible to any on board.

"Speak English!" Lord Hastings called back. "I can't understand you."

The next words came in halting English.

"Who are you?"

"British submarine, D-16!" Lord Hastings called back.

"Then why did you fire at us?"

"We didn't. You were fired upon by a German submarine, which we have just sunk. Will you come aboard?"

"Yes," was the reply, and the little boat drew closer.

A moment later a man in the uniform of the Russian navy stepped over the side and advanced toward Lord Hastings.

"Are you the commander of this vessel?" he asked.

Lord Hastings bowed.

"I am," he replied.

"Then I demand to know, as you claim, and appear, to be English, why you fired upon us?"

"I told you," said Lord Hastings quietly, "that we did not fire upon you. You were attacked by a German submarine, which we have just had the pleasure of sending to the bottom."

The Russian officer looked skeptical.

"May I ask to see your papers?" he asked.

"You may," replied Lord Hastings, now somewhat nettled, "but you won't."

"In that event," replied the officer, "I must place you under arrest."

Lord Hastings smiled sardonically.

"Which would be quite a task," he said. "Remember, you are aboard my ship now, and if I choose, I can have you thrown into the sea. However, as there seems to be some misunderstanding, I am ready to accompany you aboard your ship, where I shall explain matters to your commander."

The officer could but be satisfied with this.

"Very well," he said.

Lord Hastings turned to Jack.

"You shall go with me," he said. "Frank, you remain here."

He stepped into the boat and Jack and the Russian officer followed him. The boat put off toward the Russian cruiser.

Aboard the cruiser Lord Hastings was at once ushered into the presence of the Russian commander, Captain Bergoff. To him he told the same story he had related to his officer.

"Then how did you get in the Baltic Sea?" asked the Russian officer.

"Through the Kiel canal," replied Lord Hastings.

The Russian commander smiled.

"And you expect me to believe that?" he said. "Impossible."

"Nevertheless," said Lord Hastings, drawing himself up, "it is true."

"I won't dispute you," was the reply. "Have your own way. However, I fear that I must place you under arrest."

"Under arrest!"

"Yes. I have no doubt that you are English, but I believe you are traitors to your country. Your speech proves you are English, but it would be impossible for a British vessel to force a passage of the Kiel canal. I suppose you will tell me, however, that you sank several German vessels there."

"We did," replied Jack, breaking into the conversation for the first time.

Again the Russian smiled.

"And here seem to be two full grown men asking me to believe a thing like that," he said. "It's too much. Lieutenant!"

The officer who had escorted the two aboard approached.

"Have them confined in irons," was the command.

"But," protested Lord Hastings, "regardless of our nationality, we came here under a flag of truce."

"Spies in British uniforms," said the Russian sternly. "You will leave here under the Russian flag and in irons."

CHAPTER XVII.
PETROGRAD.

Lord Hastings stepped close to the Russian commander.

"You will interfere with us at your peril," he said quietly. "We are all that we represent ourselves to be, as you could plainly see if you were not so thick headed."

"What!" exclaimed the Russian. "You insult me? Take them away."

"One moment," said Lord Hastings, raising a hand. "First it would be well if you were to allow me to inform the officer in command of my submarine what has happened, for when we fail to go back, he is likely to believe that you are a German and sink you."

"We escaped your torpedoes before, we can do it again," said the Russian.

"I have told you," said Lord Hastings calmly, "that we are not the same submarine that pursued you. You don't believe it. Very well. However, you will learn that you cannot run away from us as you did the other."

"We shall see," said the Russian.

"Oh, you'll see, all right," said Lord Hastings. "However, we are here and that's all there is about it. Now, if you will not have us confined, we promise to make no attempt to escape."

The Russian considered this proposal for some minutes.

"Very well," he said at last. "I shall accept your paroles. See that you do not attempt to break them."

He turned and went on deck.

Five minutes later and the Russian cruiser had come about and was heading east once more. Gradually she gathered headway, until she was traveling at full speed.

The Russian kept close watch on the D-16, which now lay to the rear. And as the cruiser began to draw away, the D-16, which had been lying idle, also came to life, and started in pursuit.

Frank, aboard the submarine, was greatly puzzled when the cruiser came about and started off toward the east.

"Wonder what on earth the reason is?" he muttered to himself. "Well, I suppose we had better go along also."

He gave the signal and the D-16 started in pursuit.

Frank held a consultation with the German prisoner.

"I believe," said the latter, "that the Russian has refused to accept your commander's explanation and has had him and his first officer placed under arrest."

"By Jove!" said Frank. "I hadn't thought of that. I wouldn't be surprised if you are right."

He gave the order for full speed ahead, and gradually the submarine began to overhaul the Russian cruiser. As he came nearer, Frank perceived signs of action aboard the larger vessel, and then he was hailed across the water.

"Sheer off, or we shall fire into you."

"Don't you try it," cried Frank, angrily. "Where is my commander?"

"He is a prisoner," came back the reply, "and has given his parole not to escape."

"Let me speak to him," demanded Frank.

When this command was taken to the Russian commander, he hesitated. But at length he decided to allow Lord Hastings to hail the D-16.

"What's the matter, sir?" asked Frank, when his commander's voice reached him across the water.

Lord Hastings explained.

"But what shall I do, sir?" asked Frank.

"Just follow us. That's the best thing that can be done under the circumstances," replied Lord Hastings.

"All right," said Frank, and the conversation ended.

The Russian commander, who had listened to this conversation, still was unconvinced, and he said to Lord Hastings:

"I would advise that you have the submarine keep away, for if she comes too close we shall sink her."

Lord Hastings made no reply.

All the afternoon the Russian cruiser continued her eastward journey, the D-16 trailing behind at a considerable distance.

It was five o'clock.

Came a cry from the lookout aboard the Russian cruiser.

"Cruiser off the port bow!"

Instantly all was haste and bustle aboard the war vessel.

"German cruiser!" came the next cry, and it was followed immediately by the cry of the Russian commander:

"Clear for action!"

"Now," said Jack to Lord Hastings, "we shall see how the Russians fight."

In spite of the fact that the ship bearing down on them appeared to be much larger, the Russian commander determined to give battle, and this, too, in face of his belief that one of the enemy's submarines was trailing him.

At last the vessels came within range. A shell from the German struck the Russian squarely in the bow, cutting a deep hole and sending up a cloud of splinters, which, falling, laid three men low.

The first three Russian shells went wild.

"Rotten," said Lord Hastings.

"I should say so," agreed Jack. "Now — —"

He broke off suddenly, for at that moment, chancing to glance back, he saw the D-16, half a mile to stern, disappear from sight.

"The fight won't last long now," he said to his commander.

"Why?" demanded the latter.

"Because the D-16 is going into action."

"By Jove!" exclaimed Lord Hastings. "If Frank just acts quickly enough."

"He will, never fear," said Jack quietly.

Still the battle raged. Shells fell aboard the Russian cruiser with great regularity now. Men lay wounded and bleeding upon the deck, in the turrets, and in the engine room, where one German shell had penetrated.

But the Germans had not escaped. The Russians, once they had found the range, poured a veritable hail of shells aboard the enemy. The forward turret guns of the German were silenced by a shell that struck the revolving structure squarely and destroyed it.

For half an hour the battle raged, and then, suddenly, there came terrible cries from aboard the German, carrying plainly over the water to the ears of the Russians.

"Submarine!" came the cry. "We have been torpedoed!"

The fight was over. German sailors, those of them who were able, sprang into the sea by the dozens. Others attempted to launch the life boats. And while this was going on, there came a terrific explosion from aboard the enemy, and she sprang into flame, lighting up the semi-darkness for miles around.

Lord Hastings turned to the Russian commander, who passed him at that moment.

"You have my submarine to thank for this victory," he said quietly.

The Russian bowed gravely, and replied:

"I know it. I have treated you badly. I am sorry. However, I am willing to answer for my actions, for I had the good of my country at heart."

Lord Hastings stretched forth a hand.

"I am sure of it," he said simply. "I bear no ill will."

The Russian shook his hand heartily; then turned to the work of looking after the dead and wounded. Lord Hastings and Jack turned their eyes toward the German cruiser, which was slowly sinking.

Hundreds of German sailors were in the sea, clinging to such pieces of débris as came to hand. Immediately the Russians launched life boats and set about the work of rescue; and all who were in the water were saved, the German commander among them.

Then the German cruiser sank; and as she disappeared from sight, at a point not half a mile distant, another form appeared upon the surface. It was the D-16.

The Russian commander, who stood near at that moment, turned to Lord Hastings.

"I shall be pleased," he said, "to have you sent back aboard your ship immediately. Or I shall be still better pleased to have you accompany me, as my guests, to Petrograd, for which port I am bound."

Lord Hastings turned to Jack.

"What do you say?" he said. "Would you like to see Petrograd—or St. Petersburg, as it was called before the outbreak of the war?"

"Very much, sir," replied the lad, "if Frank can come along."

"I guess that can be managed," was the reply.

Lord Hastings turned to the Russian commander.

"Is there a safe place where I may leave my submarine?" he asked.

"It shall follow us, and be one of us," was the reply.

"In that case," said Lord Hastings, "we shall be glad to accompany you."

The Russian bowed.

"Then," said Lord Hastings, "if we may trouble you to set us aboard our own vessel, we shall follow you at a respectable distance. Besides, I should be pleased to have you come aboard, for I can promise to show you such a submarine as it has never been your pleasure to see before."

"I shall accept that offer with pleasure," replied the Russian.

Calling his first officer, he ordered that a boat be lowered, into which they all stepped and were soon upon the bridge of the D-16.

Frank received his commander and his chum with unfeigned delight, for he had been greatly worried about them.

"It was all my fault," the Russian commander said. "As your commander told me, I was thick-headed. I am sorry."

"Say no more about it," declared Lord Hastings. "Mistakes will happen."

All descended below, and, the Russian commander expressing a desire to go beneath the sea, the D-16 submerged.

Then Lord Hastings conducted the Russian on a tour of inspection of the vessel, and explained its mysteries to him. The Russian was charmed, and all sat and talked long into the night.

It was almost noon of the second day when the D-16, still following in the wake of the Russian cruiser, anchored in the harbor of Petrograd.

"I shall be pleased," said Lord Hastings, "to pay my respects to Czar Nicholas."

"I fear," said the Russian, "it may be impossible, for he is very busy these days with affairs of state."

"Nevertheless," said Lord Hastings, "I have his command to always present myself when in Russia."

"In that case," said the Russian, "it is, of course, different."

"And this time," said Lord Hastings, "I shall present to his majesty my first officer, Mr. Templeton, and my second officer, Mr. Chadwick."

CHAPTER XVIII.
A PLOT.

"What do you suppose that fellow is sneaking along like that for?" asked Jack.

Frank shrugged his shoulders.

"Search me," he replied.

The object of the lads' conversation was hurrying furtively along one of the narrow streets of the Russian capital, casting occasional glances about him.

It was the afternoon of the day following that upon which they had reached Petrograd, and Frank and Jack, together with Lord Hastings, had only just come from the palace, where they had been given an audience with the Czar. Upon leaving the palace Lord Hastings had been for returning aboard the D-16 immediately, but the lads had expressed a desire to see something of the city, and had set out by themselves. The only instructions Lord Hastings had given them was to be aboard before dark.

"Well," said Jack, still eyeing the little man slinking along the street, "I'm sure that fellow is up to something. I'd like to know what."

"I suppose the easiest way to find out," said Frank, "is to follow him."

"That suits me," replied Jack. "Come on."

A hundred yards behind they set out in pursuit of the suspect.

"What's that thing he is carrying under his arm?" asked Frank.

"Looks like it might be a bomb."

Frank laughed.

"Not much danger of that," he said.

"Oh, I don't know," was the reply. "I have read enough about Russia and St. Petersburg to believe that all the nihilists and anarchists are not dead yet."

"Well, I think you have this one spotted wrong. Look at him. He wouldn't have the nerve to carry a bomb, much less throw one."

"You can't judge a man's nerve by his looks," said Jack quietly.

"Perhaps not always," agreed Frank. "But I believe I am right in this case, at least."

"All right, but we'll have to look sharp or he'll lose us. There he goes around the corner. Hurry up."

The lads quickened their steps and rounded the corner just in time to see the man they were pursuing disappear in a little shop. Approaching closer they perceived the place to be a tobacconist's, and they also entered.

The shop keeper eyed them keenly, and to avoid any suspicion Frank bought a package of cigarettes. Then they went out.

"Did you see him?" asked Jack.

"I thought I caught a glimpse of him in the little room in the rear of the shop," replied Frank.

"I am sure it was he," agreed Jack. "He poked his head out just as I glanced in that direction."

"Well, what are we going to do about it?"

"I don't know that there is anything to do. In the first place we probably are on a wild goose chase and I fail to see why we should bother with him any longer."

"Nor I. Still I am curious."

"My curiosity is not entirely satisfied either. What do you say? Shall we let him go or shall we try and get in and see what it's all about?"

"Well," said Frank, "we have followed him this far. We might as well stay for the finish, whatever it may be."

"All right, then. Let's see if we can get in."

Two doors away from the tobacco shop a narrow alleyway led toward the rear. Making certain that no one was watching them, the boys slunk into this and made their way to the rear of the shop.

Here they looked around carefully. Not a soul was in sight. Near by stood a barrel. Frank dragged it close to a little window in the room behind the shop and while Jack stood on guard, Frank climbed up and peered in.

The blind was drawn, but it did not reach the bottom by an inch. The opening was just level with Frank's eyes when he stood upon the barrel.

He looked in, exercising the greatest care to avoid detection. His eyes beheld a strange sight.

Gathered about a little table in the room were four men, their heads close together, scrutinizing an object that lay between them. At first Frank could not make out what it was, but as one of the men leaned back in his chair, Frank, over his shoulder, recognized it.

Quickly he jumped from the barrel and whispered to Jack.

"You were right."

"Right? How?" asked Jack.

"Bomb," replied Frank briefly.

Jack stepped back in surprise.

"A bomb!" he exclaimed.

"Yes," Frank repeated, "a bomb. They are examining it, or something. I can't tell just what."

"Couldn't you hear what they were saying?"

"No; the window is closed."

"What do you suppose they intend to do with it?"

"You know as much about it as I do."

"Well, then, what are we going to do about it?"

"That's the question. I suppose we might call the police, but if we did the chances are they would find nothing when they entered the place; or we might notify the military authorities, but the conspirators would be gone before they arrived."

"Haven't you an idea?"

"Yes, I have an idea, but it involves considerable risk."

"Since when have you become so cautious? Risk didn't use to bother you."

"It wouldn't now, if I were sure we had a chance of success."

"What's your plan?"

"There is but one way I can think of by which we can overhear the conversation in that room. It is impossible for us to get in this way without being seen, and the only other entrance, so far as I know, is through the tobacco shop. Therefore we shall have to go in that way."

"And I suppose the shopkeeper will stand right there and let us do it," said Jack with some sarcasm.

"We'll have to tie him up before he can give the alarm."

"Suits me," said Jack. "I am willing to take a chance if you are. Come on."

Quickly the lads made their way back to the street, and once more entered the store. The shopkeeper recognized them instantly by their uniforms, and approached.

"These cigarettes you gave me," said Frank, "are no good. I want another package."

"What's the matter with them?" demanded the storekeeper. "Let me see them."

Frank laid the package in his hand, and as the latter turned his eyes down to look at the package, Frank seized him about the throat with both hands. Jack picked up a strong piece of cord from the floor, and bound the man's hands securely, while Frank kept him from making an outcry. Making a gag of his handkerchief, he stuffed it into the man's mouth in such a way that it was impossible for him to utter a sound. Then they laid him behind the counter on the floor.

"Now we shall see what we can hear," said Frank.

He approached the door to the next room noiselessly, Jack close at his heels. For a few minutes they waited in silence, but there was no sound from the adjoining room. At last Frank ventured to peer in. He stepped back in astonishment.

"Gone!" he exclaimed.

"Gone," repeated Jack.

"Yes; and I would like to know where."

"Let's go in and see."

Their hands rested upon their revolvers as they advanced into the room and looked about. From one end to the other they searched, when as they were about to give up, Frank discovered a door behind some old barrels in the far corner.

"Here is where they went," he whispered.

He tried the door, and it gave way before him, though not until he had used considerable force. A pair of stairs, going down, confronted them.

"Shall we go down or not?" asked Frank, turning to Jack.

"Suit yourself," was the reply. "I'm with you either way."

Without another word Frank turned about and began to descend the stairs, taking care to make no noise. Jack followed him.

At the bottom, where it was pitch dark, they brought up against a second door, and making sure that his revolvers were ready for instant use, Frank pushed it gently.

It swung open.

Seated about a table were the figures of four men. Fortunately for the boys, perhaps, their backs were toward the door, and they did not see it open.

Motioning to Jack to follow, Frank crept in quietly and as quietly sank behind a pile of old boxes in the nearest corner. Jack did likewise, and the two made themselves as comfortable as possible, without making a sound, for there was no telling how long they might have to remain there.

Kneeling, Jack poked up his head until he could just see over the top of the barrel. One of the men made some remark, but it was in Russian, and neither lad could understand what he said. No sooner had he spoken, however, than a second man turned on him angrily.

"I thought we had agreed to speak English," he said. "Of course it makes no difference here, but practice is good for you. Unless you get used to speaking English you are likely to make a slip the first thing you know in some place where it will spoil everything."

"You are right," said the first speaker. "I shall try to be more careful."

"See that you do," growled the second speaker.

"Well," said a third voice, "this thing seems to be all right. Now about the time."

"We have decided upon that," said the fourth man. "Czar Nicholas will review his troops before the palace at five o'clock. Ivan and I can get close enough for him to throw with accuracy."

"Good. Has it been decided that Ivan is to do the work?"

"Yes."

"All right. Then we may as well go. Remember, do not speak to Stephan as you go out. It might spoil everything."

The men arose, and made their way from the room, without noticing the lads.

The latter, being sure they were gone, arose to their feet and followed.

"Careful," whispered Frank, as they ascended the stairs.

CHAPTER XIX.
THE PLOTTERS FOILED.

When the conspirators passed through the tobacco shop they did not even glance toward the counter, and therefore did not notice the absence of the shopkeeper. Had they done so, there probably would have been a different story to tell.

Frank and Jack, once outside the store, breathed easier, and followed the conspirators at what they deemed a safe distance, nevertheless keeping close enough upon their heels not to lose sight of them should they turn into some place suddenly.

"Lucky for us they didn't see what we did to the proprietor of that shop," said Jack.

"I should say so," replied Frank.

"Now if we can just keep close enough without being discovered," said Frank, "we may be able to find some means of preventing this tragedy."

"If they don't stop some place, we are all right," agreed Frank.

Jack looked at his watch.

"By Jove!" he ejaculated.

"What's the matter?" asked Frank.

"Why, it's after four o'clock now. There is not much time. Evidently we must be closer to the palace than I thought."

"Well, the sooner this is over the better I shall be pleased."

"Not losing your nerve, are you?"

"Not exactly; still I feel a little uncomfortable."

Turning off the narrow side street, the lads followed the men down a much busier thoroughfare, where, at the far end, they could see a great crowd gathered. The men made directly for it, and, approaching closer, the lads recognized the Czar's palace.

Right through the large crowd gathered about, the four men pushed their way; then, abruptly they separated into pairs.

Jack grasped Frank by the arm.

"Quick!" he exclaimed. "You follow those two," pointing, "and I'll take the others. We don't know which one has the bomb."

Frank nodded and set out in pursuit of the two moving toward the left.

In the crowd there was little danger that the men would notice that they were being followed, and Frank felt safe in crowding right on behind them. Jack followed the same plan with the other pair.

The crowd was held back by long lines of troops on either side of the street, spectators not being permitted closer than a hundred feet of the line of march.

In the extreme front, where they forced their way by dint of much pushing and shoving, the conspirators took their stand. Frank glanced about. Perhaps a hundred yards down the line he thought he caught sight of the large stature of his friend, but of this he could not be positive.

Half an hour passed, then three quarters, then the sound of a distant bugle and galloping hoofs gave notice that the troops were approaching. Almost at the same moment a figure descended the palace steps and mounted a large black charger. The figure was handsomely garbed, and gold glittered over his uniform. Even from where he stood Frank could make out that he wore a beard.

It was Nicholas Romanoff, Czar of all the Russias.

The Czar rode his horse slowly down the lane of spectators and Frank and Jack, each in his respective place, became tense, expectant and ready for instant action.

Suddenly one of the men near Frank made a move and the lad half drew his revolver. The man simply produced a handkerchief, however, and wiped beads of perspiration from his brow. Frank thrust his revolver back in his pocket, but kept his hand upon it.

The Czar, riding slowly, drew near to where Jack and the other two conspirators stood. Then it was that Jack recognized that he was the one who held the Czar's life in his hands.

The conspirator to his left thrust his hand under his coat and drew forth a round dark object, which he concealed from the crowd. Jack's sharp eyes had seen the move, but he did not act yet.

Now the Czar was directly abreast them, not more than a hundred feet away.

Slowly the conspirator drew back his hand, and in another instant would have hurled the bomb upon the Czar; but at that moment Jack came to life.

As the man drew back his arm, Jack stepped quickly forward, and, seizing the upraised hand in both his, wrenched the arm violently. The man staggered back with a cry of pain, and dropped the bomb.

But before it could touch the ground, where it would undoubtedly have exploded, killing and maiming many, Jack slipped one hand beneath it and caught it gently.

Then the two thwarted conspirators sprang upon him.

There seemed to be no one in the crowd who had perceived the cause of Jack's struggle with the two men, and the latter, taking advantage of this fact, struggled fiercely with Jack, uttering loud cries of "Assassin!" "Kill him!" "He tried to assassinate the Czar!"

With his one free hand, Jack fought desperately, but the crowd, attracted by the cries of the two conspirators, closed in on him angrily. Some one wrenched the bomb from his hand, and other hands clawed and struck at his face and body.

Jack fought back gamely, for he realized that if once knocked to the ground he would probably be killed before the authorities could intervene to save him. He struck out vigorously right and left and men fell before his terrific blows.

But the odds were too great and were bound to tell at last. Jack went down, and the crowd piled on top of him.

At that instant a troop of horsemen bore down upon the struggling heap, striking right and left with their sabres and scattering the crowd in all directions, and they arrived none too soon.

Jack was unconscious. Bleeding from knife wounds in half a dozen places, and his face covered with blood from a wound in the forehead where a missile of some kind had struck, he lay perfectly helpless.

Rough soldier hands lifted him rudely from the ground and flung him across a horse, and then the troop galloped away.

While all this was going on, Frank had tried in vain to reach the side of his friend, who he knew was in trouble of some kind, although he could not make sure what. He did not realize the true state of affairs until he had seen the troopers take his friend's body from beneath many others.

"Great Scott!" he cried to himself then. "They believe Jack tried to kill the Czar! What shall I do?"

The answer to this question came to him like a flash. Lord Hastings, a personal friend of the Czar, was, perhaps, the only man who, under the circumstances, would be given a hearing. Frank turned quickly and dashed madly down the street.

Round corner after corner he ran at full speed, nor did he check his stride until he reached the harbor and the spot near where the submarine D-16 was anchored.

A man with a rowboat hustled up at Frank's bidding, and the lad ordered him to pull for the submarine with all speed.

Jumping aboard and bidding the rower to wait for him, Frank dashed madly for Lord Hastings' quarters.

The commander of the D-16 rose quickly to his feet as his door was thrown violently open and Frank, gasping for breath and with pale face, stood before him.

"What's the matter?" demanded Lord Hastings anxiously.

"Jack—Jack—arrested," panted Frank.

Lord Hastings drew close and took him by the shoulders.

"Take your time," he said quietly. "Nothing was ever gained by too great haste. Get your breath and then tell me what the trouble is."

For another half a minute Frank gasped on, then finally was able to speak more calmly.

"Jack has been arrested," he said.

"What for?" asked Lord Hastings calmly.

"He's accused of trying to assassinate the Czar."

"What!" cried Lord Hastings, staggering back and almost losing his composure.

"It's true, sir," cried Frank.

"By George, this is serious!" said Lord Hastings. "Now tell me all about it as quickly as you can."

Frank did so, and Lord Hastings listened quietly until he had concluded. Then he quickly got his hat and coat, and motioning to Frank to follow, made his way to the bridge. Both climbed into the boat that had brought Frank aboard the submarine and the rower put off for shore with powerful strokes.

"Is Jack in much danger, sir?" asked Frank.

"I don't know," said Lord Hastings. "In times of peace, of course, he would be given a trial; but the anger of the people and the troopers now will be so great that it is hard to say what will happen."

"Where are we going, sir?"

"First to the chief of police; then to the Czar himself."

Lord Hastings, who knew the Russian police chief well, had no difficulty in gaining admittance, and Frank with him. To the chief Frank told his story. The chief appeared somewhat incredulous.

"I have not the slightest doubt of your integrity, Lord Hastings," he said, "but may you not be mistaken in your officers?"

"I am not mistaken," said Lord Hastings stiffly. "Now, I want to know at once what action you will take to release my friend at once."

"There is nothing I can do," said the chief. "The prisoner has been taken out of my hands by the military authorities. I am afraid you must appeal to the Czar, and I am not at all sure that such an appeal will result favorably to you."

"Then I have no time to lose here," said Lord Hastings abruptly, and made for the door, Frank following him.

At the door of the palace Lord Hastings demanded an audience of the Czar immediately.

"It is impossible, my lord," said the attendant. "His majesty is engaged in the case of his attempted assassination and cannot be disturbed."

"But I must see his majesty at once," said Lord Hastings hotly, "and it is of this very case I would consult him."

"I am very sorry — —"

Lord Hastings suddenly produced his revolver.

"I am a friend of his majesty's," he said, very quietly, "and you will either tell him this instant that I desire an audience in connection with this case, or I shall push my way in over your dead body! This is a matter of life and death and I am not to be trifled with!"

CHAPTER XX.
BOUND WESTWARD AGAIN.

Again the attendant started to protest, but Lord Hastings, taking a step forward, pushed him violently backward with his right hand and walked on. In vain did the attendant walk after him, trying to halt him. Lord Hastings paid no heed to his words, and Frank followed close at his heels.

Then, perceiving that words were of no value, the attendant suddenly produced a revolver.

"My lord," he said quietly, "one more step and you are a dead man."

Before Lord Hastings could reply Frank had sprung upon the attendant and wrested the revolver from his hand. The latter sent up a loud cry and footsteps immediately could be heard hurrying toward them.

Half a dozen soldiers entered the room and surrounded the struggling knot of men. An officer gave a command:

"Shoot them!"

Rifles were brought to bear, and just as it seemed that the two were about to be shot down, another figure, attracted by the sounds of confusion, entered the room.

"Hold!" he exclaimed to the officer, and the soldiers lowered their rifles.

"What is the meaning of this confusion in my palace?" asked the Czar, for it was he, angrily. "Why this unseemly noise?"

Suddenly his eyes fell upon Lord Hastings.

"Lord Hastings!" he exclaimed in surprise. "What brings you here, and what is the meaning of this fighting? If my people have been discourteous to you they shall answer for it," and the Czar gazed about him angrily.

The eyes of all fell before him.

Czar Nicholas advanced and took Lord Hastings by the hand.

"Of what service can I be to you?" he asked. "And will you kindly tell me the cause of this trouble? My own subjects seem to be tongue-tied."

"The cause of the trouble, your majesty," said Lord Hastings, "is that one of your attendants refused to tell your majesty that I desired an audience immediately, on a matter of life and death."

"So!" exclaimed the Czar. "They shall answer for it. But I have been engaged already in some such matter. An attempt was made to assassinate me not an hour ago."

"So I have been told," said Lord Hastings, "and it is concerning that that I would speak."

"And what do you know about it?" asked the Czar in surprise.

"Only, your Majesty, that you have the wrong man."

The Czar took a step back.

"That is what the prisoner says," he replied drily. "But what do you know of this matter?"

"Your prisoner," said Lord Hastings, "is one of the lads I presented to you this morning, my own first officer."

"By Jove!" said the Czar in perfect English, "I thought his face looked familiar. So it is he, eh? Well, if he did not try to kill me how does it come that he was seen with the bomb in his hand?"

Frank stepped forward.

"I can explain that, if your majesty will give me permission," he said quietly.

The Czar looked at him.

"And you," he said, "are Lord Hastings' second officer, are you not?"

"I am, your majesty."

"Then tell me what you know of this attempted assassination, if anything."

As briefly as possible Frank reconstructed the scene for the Czar. As he progressed with his tale, the Czar became more and more interested.

116

"And so," Frank concluded, "had it not been for my friend, who your majesty is pleased to believe would have killed him, the real assassin would have accomplished his work."

"You tell exactly the same story as the prisoner," said the Czar thoughtfully. "There must be truth in it."

"I can vouch for both of them, your majesty," interposed Lord Hastings. "Why, time after time they have been instrumental in dealing smashing blows to the enemy. Do you believe, then, that one of them would attempt to murder the ruler of one of England's allies?"

The Czar struck the table violently with his clenched fist.

"No!" he shouted. "I don't believe it. The lad is innocent, and he shall be freed immediately, no matter what my counselors may have to say."

He called for his chief aide, and to that worthy gave the command:

"Have the prisoner brought before me at once."

"But, your majesty — —" began the aide.

The Czar turned on him angrily.

"There are no buts!" he exclaimed. "Have him brought here immediately — immediately, do you understand?"

The aide saluted and left the room hurriedly.

The Czar turned to Frank.

"And can you lead my men to the rendezvous where this plot was hatched?" he asked.

"Yes, your majesty," replied Frank.

"Good. Then, perhaps as they are unaware that their rendezvous has been discovered, they may be captured."

Frank bowed.

Perhaps five minutes later the Czar's chief aide returned, followed by Jack, still looking very weak and shaky as the result of his experiences of a few hours. Motioning to the others in the room to remain silent, the Czar advanced and addressed Jack.

"So," he exclaimed in a harsh voice, "you are the man who tried to kill me, eh?"

"No, your majesty," replied Jack, "I— —"

The Czar silenced him with a gesture.

"Oh, I know your excuse," he said. "Your friends have interceded for you, and I have every confidence in Lord Hastings. Of you, however, I know nothing. A hundred people saw you with the bomb in your hand. The case is perfectly plain."

"But," began Jack.

"Silence!" exclaimed the Czar, raising a hand.

He turned to his aide again.

"Bring me," he commanded, "the small velvet box on my writing desk."

He turned and addressed all in the room as the aide hurried away.

"You shall all see," he exclaimed, "how I dispose of a case like this."

There was silence until the aide returned, and put the little box in the Czar's hand.

Concealing the contents from Jack, the Czar opened it and took out something. Then he commanded:

"Approach!"

Jack did so, and with his left hand the Czar took him by the right shoulder, while with his right he touched him over the heart; and when Jack stepped back and his fingers touched the spot where the Czar's had rested so lightly he felt something pinned thereon. Examining it he found it to be The Cross of St. George.

He had been decorated by the Czar himself for personal gallantry.

"Your majesty— —" stammered Jack, and fell upon his knee.

The Czar stretched forth his right hand, which Jack bent over and touched with his lips.

"There, there," said the Czar, with the suspicion of huskiness in his voice. "I shouldn't have fooled you so, but I simply could not resist. Mr. Templeton, you are a brave lad, and I envy my friend Lord Hastings the possession of so gallant an officer."

Lord Hastings and Frank both now approached Jack and shook hands with him. Jack smiled faintly.

"I thought it was all over with me," he said as he turned to Frank. "Of course," he added, "I knew you would do all you possibly could for me, but I was afraid you couldn't do enough, and you, too. Lord Hastings."

"Now," said the Czar, "if you will lead my men to the spot where you discovered the plot, I shall appreciate it."

The lads signified their willingness to obey this command, and some minutes later, with a squad of mounted troops they drew rein at the tobacco shop.

The door was closed, and a knock brought no response. One of the soldiers burst in the door with the toe of his boot and all entered. They ransacked the place from top to bottom, but could find no one.

"When they came back and found the storekeeper bound, they released him and all moved," said Frank.

"That's about the size of it," Jack agreed. "They knew when they found him that their rendezvous had been discovered."

"They have left no clue," said the Russian officer in command, "so there is nothing to be done. Come, we shall go."

They returned to the palace, where the Czar insisted on having Lord Hastings, Frank and Jack dine with him.

This they did, and at a late hour returned aboard the D-16.

"And which way shall we go now?" asked Frank.

"Well," said Lord Hastings, "I had thought of going back the way we came."

"Suits me," said Jack. "Of course there is considerable action over here, but I am not particularly fond of the brand. I would rather get back on the other side."

"As long as we are practically free agents," said Frank, "I have a plan to propose."

"And that is?" asked Lord Hastings.

"Well, it probably will be weeks before the allied ships are able to force a passage of the Dardanelles, and with our speed, we can reach there long before that. See what I mean?"

Lord Hastings smiled.

"I see," he replied briefly.

"And what do you think of the plan?"

"I am in favor of it," said Jack.

"And so am I," declared Lord Hastings. "But, remember, to get there quickly we shall once more have to pass through the Kiel canal."

"We did it once. We can do it again," replied Frank quietly.

CHAPTER XXI.
A NEUTRALITY VIOLATION.

Through the Gulf of Finland into the Baltic the D-16 made her way rapidly, remaining upon the surface of the water, for in these seas there was no danger of encountering an enemy. Some miles from the mouth of the Kiel canal, however, Lord Hastings gave the command to submerge, and the little submarine, sinking gently, hurried on, at a somewhat reduced speed, but making good time nevertheless.

On this second passage of the canal, Lord Hastings decided to make no raid upon the enemy's fleet cooped up within it, and accordingly the D-16, running close to the bottom, guided by Lord Hastings' own hand, made the trip in safety, without encountering a single one of the enemy's under-the-sea fighters. However, she did not rise immediately when she was once more in the North Sea, for these waters were mined for miles, and it was necessary for the D-16 to pass under the mined area before coming again to the surface.

But, going more swiftly now, the British submarine soon reached a zone of comparative safety and Lord Hastings gave the command to come to the surface once more. Then, followed by Frank and Jack, he stepped on to the bridge for a breath of the cool air.

"Well, I was sure we would get through safely, and we have," said Jack, as he peered off across the water.

"And we have accomplished," said Lord Hastings, "such a feat as was never before attempted, and one that has been rated as impossible. You lads are both deserving of the greatest praise for your coolness and bravery."

"No more than our commander, I am sure," replied Frank quietly. "Had it not been for you, the trip never could have been made."

"But," said his commander, "had it not been for you lads, the trip would never have been thought of."

"Well," said Frank with a laugh, "we'll call it square all around and let it go at that."

"Suits me," declared Lord Hastings, also laughing.

"It seems to me," said Jack, "that the crew is just as deserving of praise."

"So they are," said Lord Hastings, "and I shall see that their names are given special mention in my report to the Admiralty."

"Which reminds me," said Frank, "that we still have the German prisoner aboard."

"By Jove!" exclaimed Lord Hastings. "Do you know I had forgotten all about him?"

"What do you intend to do with him?" asked Frank.

"Well," said Lord Hastings slowly, "I had intended giving him his liberty at the first opportunity. So far none has presented itself. If something doesn't turn up soon, I fear I shall have to turn him over to the Dover military authorities as a prisoner of war."

Jack gave vent to an expressive whistle.

"After what you have told him," he said, "that will make it rather hard."

"So it will," admitted his commander, "but if half a chance turns up I shall see that he is set free. For had it not been for him, Frank, you would probably be imprisoned in Berlin right now."

"That is undoubtedly true," said Frank, "and I am properly grateful."

"We'll see," said Lord Hastings, and this put an end, for the time being, to the subject.

Still running at full speed upon the surface, the D-16 was making rapid headway toward the British coast.

"We had best be careful, sir," said Jack. "Remember what the prisoner told us about the submarine blockade."

"Right," was the reply. "Of course there is a safety zone for the protection of neutral ships, but as we do not know just where these fellows are likely to be hanging about, we had better take a stitch in time and go down a ways."

He turned to give the command, but before the words could leave his lips, he turned suddenly again at a cry from Frank.

"What's up now?" he demanded.

For answer Frank pointed straight ahead toward the distant horizon.

"Looks like a ship in some kind of trouble, sir."

Lord Hastings raised his glass to his eyes and peered through it long and intently.

"She's in distress, that's sure," he said, lowering the glass at last. "But I can't make her out from this distance. She doesn't look like a ship of war, though."

"Probably some merchantman victim of the German submarine blockade," said Jack.

"That's about the size of it," Frank agreed.

"Well," said Lord Hastings, "we'll go closer and see, although there is nothing we can do for them."

The object of this conversation lay almost due west, a trifle north. The head of the D-16 was consequently turned slightly, and she made for the vessel at top speed. The three officers remained upon the bridge, barely rising above the water, and at last they were able to make out the ship.

"Merchantman, all right!" said Jack.

"Yes!" exclaimed Frank, becoming suddenly excited, "and do you make out her colors?"

Jack took another look.

"By Jove!" he exclaimed.

Lord Hastings also raised his glass to his eyes again, then started back with an exclamation of surprise.

"They have gone too far this time," he said slowly. "This means trouble."

For the colors flying at the masthead of the sinking merchant ship were the Stars and Stripes!

"The United States will not let them get away with anything like that," declared Frank vehemently.

"Don't be too sure," replied Lord Hastings. "Remember the incident of the firing of Turkish forts upon an American battleship launch at Beirut. Nothing came of that."

"But," protested Frank, "it is inconceivable that the United States will not take action if a German submarine has sent one of her merchant ships to the bottom."

"Looks like an act of war to me," said Jack.

"Germany will probably claim," said Lord Hastings, "that the ship did not stay within the established safety channel, or else deny that a German submarine is responsible."

"She might do the latter," said Frank, "but I don't believe the United States would accept the former explanation."

But the United States eventually did, as it developed later, although she lodged a formal protest through her ambassador at Berlin.

"B-o-s-n-i-a," Frank spelled out the name of the sinking ship, as the D-16 drew closer.

"I wonder if her crew is safe?" he asked anxiously.

Lord Hastings pointed across the water.

"You can see some of them in the small boats," he said. "I hope they all get away. The submarine must have torpedoed them without warning."

"I haven't any doubt of that," said Frank, "although it is against all rules of civilized warfare."

"I do not claim that the Germans are conducting a civilized war," said Lord Hastings quietly. "The tales of cruelties coming out of Belgium augur decidedly against that."

At this juncture a fourth figure ascended to the bridge. It was that of the German prisoner.

He took in the situation at a glance, and turned to Lord Hastings with a faint smile.

"A victim of the blockade, I suppose?" he questioned.

Lord Hastings nodded.

"Looks like it," he said briefly, "and an American ship at that."

The German muttered an imprecation under his breath.

"I was afraid something like that would happen," he said. "I never was in favor with the policy of torpedoing neutral ships, whether in the blockaded zone or not. To my way of thinking, no good can come of it."

"I have an idea that no good for Germany will come from this," said Lord Hastings.

"Still," said the prisoner hopefully, "it may be all right. The United States will endeavor to stay out of the war on any pretext. Besides, she is woefully slow to act, as has been proved by her actions toward Mexico. Therefore this may be overlooked."

"Don't you believe it," cried Frank hotly. "The United States will protect her citizens and property the world over."

"Well," said the German with a scornful smile, "it's about time she began to do it."

"What do you mean?" asked Frank taking a step toward the prisoner. "Do you mean we are all cowards?"

"Well, hardly that," replied the German, with a faint smile, "but— —"

"But nothing," cried Frank. "We don't raise such things as cowards in the United States."

The German lifted his eyebrows skeptically, and Frank grew angrier.

"You'll try us too far some of these days," he said, "and we'll do you like Dewey did some of your ships at Manila. He said: 'Get out of my way and don't interfere with me or I shall send you all to the bottom.'"

The German's face flushed. Plainly he also was growing angry.

"If you try it," he said, "you'll wish you hadn't."

"Why?" demanded Frank. "Do you think you can lick us?"

"I don't think there is any question about it!" was the reply.

"Well, don't you ever fool yourselves!" exclaimed Frank angrily. "We — —"

"Here, here," exclaimed Lord Hastings at this juncture, laying a hand upon Frank's arm. "No more of this. Remember, Frank, that this man is a prisoner and should be treated courteously."

Frank drew away grumbling.

"Then he wants to let my country alone," he protested.

The German, also, would have continued the argument, but Lord Hastings settled the matter.

"Not another word of this," he said sternly, and Frank and the prisoner bowed to this command.

"There she goes," cried Lord Hastings suddenly, pointing to the sinking ship.

All gazed toward the vessel. Slowly she rose high in the air, seemed to hang in the very air for a few brief moments, then dived and the waters closed over her. The American Steamship Bosnia, torpedoed by a German submarine or shattered by a German mine, sank to the bottom of the North Sea.

CHAPTER XXII.

IN THE MEDITERRANEAN.

"And I guess we might as well sink, also," said Lord Hastings.

"Wait a moment," protested the German prisoner. "What are you going to do with me? You remember you promised me my liberty before we entered the Baltic."

"That is true," replied Lord Hastings, "but so far no opportunity has presented itself. There has been no chance to fulfill my promise."

"Well," said the prisoner, "I am willing to take a chance. Give me a boat and enough provisions for a day, and set me adrift."

"But you may not make shore that way," protested Lord Hastings.

"That will be my funeral, not yours. I am willing to take the chance. I know these waters pretty well, and if you can furnish me with a pair of oars, I will guarantee that I will find a place of safety within twenty-four hours."

Lord Hastings turned the matter over in his mind for some moments.

"So be it," he said at length. "When would you start?"

"At once."

"Mr. Templeton," said Lord Hastings, "you will have one of the small boats stocked with provisions and water sufficient for twenty-four hours. We shall not submerge until our prisoner has left us."

Jack saluted.

"Very well, sir," he said, and disappeared below.

It was but the work of minutes to water and provision the small boat, and when at last all was in readiness, the boat was lowered into the sea. The prisoner climbed in and took up the oars that had been furnished him.

"Goodbye," he called to the three officers. "Thanks for your hospitality. I hope to be able to return it some of these days."

"I hope you will never have to," Lord Hastings called back. "Goodbye."

The German waved his hand in reply, and the three aboard the bridge of the D-16 waved back at him. Then he bent to his oars, and set out in a direction that, barring accident, would take him to Heligoland.

"Good luck to him," said Jack, as the German rowed away.

"The same," said Frank.

"Now," said Lord Hastings, "for that long deferred dive."

All three went below and soon the D-16 sank from sight.

There was no further incident as the D-16 wended her way along. She reached Dover Harbor without difficulty, where Lord Hastings put in to replenish his supply of coal and food. Here he also filed his report to the Admiralty. Upon the morning of the following day, the submarine pointed her nose up the English Channel toward the Atlantic Ocean.

Once upon the broad expanse of the Atlantic the D-16 turned her prow southward and ran down the coast of France at full speed, finally emerging into the sunny waters of the Mediterranean.

"I believe," said Lord Hastings, "that, on our way to the Dardanelles, we might run into the Adriatic and see what success the French fleet is having with the Austrians."

"Good," said Frank. "Ever since we left there I have been anxious to get back for a day or two."

"Suits me, too," declared Jack.

Accordingly the submarine, instead of going straight to the allied fleet off the Dardanelles, swerved at the entrance of the Adriatic, and soon was among the French fleet gathered there.

The blockade of the Austrian fleet in the Adriatic, up to this time, had been maintained with all vigilance, and in spite of several attempts of the enemy to run the blockade, they were still bottled up. What attempts they had made had been defeated with heavy losses, and it seemed that there would not be another.

There was no denying the fact that the French fleet was superior to that of the Austrians, but it was still something of a mystery to naval authorities why the Austrians did not venture forth to give battle.

True, they had done this once in the earlier stages of the war, assisted by four Zeppelin dirigibles, but they had been driven back after several of their most powerful ships had been sunk and the dirigibles hurled into the sea. After that the Austrians made no more attacks in force, but confined their operations to raids by single ships, one or two of which had been successful enough to dispose of one or two French battleships, or cruisers.

But, for weeks, now, there had been a dearth of active operations in the Adriatic. This, then, was the situation there when the D-16 moved in to spend a quiet day among the French men-of-war.

It soon proved that the day was not to be a quiet one. In fact, the D-16 had hardly time to let go her anchor, close under the lee of the French flagship, before she was engaged.

Lord Hastings, once the D-16 had anchored, went aboard the French flagship to pay his respects to the French admiral. The latter greeted him warmly, for the two, before the war, had been close friends.

"Pretty quiet, eh, admiral?" was Lord Hastings' greeting.

"Well, it has been, Hastings," was the reply, "but my nose tells me there is something in the wind. It is too all-fired quiet to suit me. This stillness spells trouble, or I miss my guess."

"Where do you get that idea?" asked Lord Hastings. "It seems to me that you have these fellows bottled up so tight that they won't make another break."

"Well, it would look that way. I suppose I base my prediction on the fact that in the Austrian admiral's place, I should take some sort of action. I know I couldn't remain bottled up like that without chafing a bit."

"Nor I," Lord Hastings admitted, "but you must remember that the Austrians are of a different breed."

"Still they have been known to fight," mused the admiral.

"Oh, yes, they have been known to fight; but, to my knowledge, they have never been known to beat anyone and I don't think they ever will."

"I have learned," said the admiral, "they have completed several submarine vessels, and I fear that they may attempt a raid beneath the water. Of course, I have my own submarines, but the enemy may get by."

"In which case," said Lord Hastings, "it is a good thing, perhaps, that I arrived just when I did."

"I fail to see," said the admiral, "how your vessel can hope to discover the enemy any easier than my own."

"Well, I'll tell you," and Lord Hastings went into a detailed account of the capabilities of the D-16, laying particular emphasis upon her huge searchlight compartment, separated from the water only by thick glass, and upon her ability to remain indefinitely under the water.

The French admiral was greatly astonished, but when Lord Hastings told him of his course and assured him that the D-16 was capable of all he claimed for her, the admiral was delighted.

"Then you may really be of assistance to me," he said.

"I shall be glad to aid in any way possible," declared Lord Hastings. "You have but to command me. Consider me under your orders for the next twenty-four hours."

"In that event," said the French admiral, "I wish that you would try and creep into the harbor and learn what is going on. 'Forewarned is forearmed,' you know."

"I shall be glad to do so."

Lord Hastings bade the admiral goodbye and returned aboard the D-16 immediately.

When Frank and Jack learned that there was work ahead of them, both at once became very enthusiastic and could hardly wait to be on their way.

"We may as well submerge right here and then advance," said Lord Hastings.

The order was given and the D-16 disappeared from the sight of the other ships. Then she moved forward slowly.

Frank, at his place in the lookout compartment, kept his eyes wide open for the sign of an enemy, or of the enemy's mines.

Suddenly a dark object appeared directly ahead of him and, swerving quickly, dashed by before he could give the alarm.

Immediately he informed Lord Hastings and the D-16 was brought about quickly and headed after the object.

"I don't know whether it is an enemy or not," said Lord Hastings, "but we can afford to take no chances. We'll have to go after it."

The D-16 dashed on, but after half an hour saw no sign of what all believed to have been an Austrian submarine.

"Might as well go up and take a look about," said Lord Hastings. "We should be among the French fleet again."

And among the French fleet they were, as they learned as soon as they bobbed up on the surface.

But now the air of quiet that had been prevalent before the D-16 submerged was changed. The peaceful appearance of the French fleet, which had been lying quietly in the water, was gone.

As the three officers stepped upon the bridge, hoarse cries of command came to their ears. Battleships began to move from their moorings, and all were cleared for action.

"Great Scott!" ejaculated Frank. "What do you suppose is the matter?"

"I don't know," said Lord Hastings, but Jack cried:

"Look!"

Lord Hastings and Frank gazed in the direction indicated, and both cried out in alarm and amazement.

Not half a mile away a French cruiser of the first class was sinking by the head. Members of her crew were throwing themselves into the sea, and boats from other ships were standing by to pick them up.

"What do you suppose is the matter? Explosion?" asked Frank.

"Looks like it," answered his commander. "I— —"

But Jack supplied the answer.

"The Austrian submarine that passed us!" he exclaimed. "She is responsible for this."

"By Jove!" exclaimed Lord Hastings. "You must be right."

At this moment the French Admiral signalled Lord Hastings.

"Torpedoed by Austrian submarine," read the signal flags.

Frank hastened to get out the D-16's flags, and in response to Lord Hastings' command, signalled the flagship:

"She escaped us, but we'll get her."

The flagship signalled "good luck" and Lord Hastings gave the command to submerge.

"Unless I am much mistaken," he said, "the Austrian will make for the open sea. Probably she will make for the Mediterranean and attempt to sink some of our merchant vessels. They may have established a base some place."

"I wouldn't be surprised if you are right, sir," said Jack. "But we'll get her."

"We will," said Lord Hastings. "We'll get her if I have to chase her around the world."

The D-16, with her periscope protruding slightly above the water, dashed on at full speed.

CHAPTER XXIII.
THE CHASE.

Lord Hastings stood at the periscope. Frank was on duty in the lookout compartment. Every man was at his post and ready for instant action. Torpedoes were in the tubes and every man stood at attention, for there was no knowing at what moment they might come upon the enemy, and Lord Hastings had no mind to allow the enemy to fire the first shot.

Suddenly, as Frank peered intently into the murky water, a blinding light dazzled his eyes; then, as suddenly, it was gone and all was black before him.

The lad immediately summoned Lord Hastings, to whom he related this strange occurrence. The latter thought some time before replying:

"There is but one possible explanation. There can be no such light beneath the sea except that furnished by the hand of man. The Austrian submarine must have some device similar to ours."

"There can be no other explanation, sir."

"And the result is that we shall have to be doubly careful," said Lord Hastings, as he returned to his post at the periscope.

Suddenly Jack, who stood near Lord Hastings, was startled to see his commander leap back and utter a loud exclamation.

"There she goes!" he cried. "Push her to the limit, Mr. Templeton."

In response to Jack's order the D-16 leaped ahead faster than before.

"Has he sighted our periscope, sir?" asked Jack.

"No, I do not think so, but for a submarine, she is moving with great speed."

"But not so fast as we are, sir?"

"I should say not quite. We appear to be gaining a trifle."

"She must be another surprise the enemy has been waiting to spring on us," said Jack.

"Undoubtedly; and the only thing that gives us the advantage is that we know about what she can do and she has no idea what we can do; in fact not even that we are here."

"But she is bound to spot us unless we submerge," said Jack.

"True," said Lord Hastings, "but if we submerge she is likely to escape us unless we use our searchlight. I would avoid letting her know we are at least on anything like even terms, if possible."

"I see, sir," said Jack. "Then the idea is to get as close as possible without being seen, and the moment we are discovered we are to dive?"

"Exactly; and if we are so fortunate as to get close enough before being seen, we will launch a torpedo immediately. But we must make the first one count, or we may get the worst of it."

Lord Hastings ceased talking and peered intently into the periscope.

"Ten minutes more undiscovered," he said, "and we will have him."

Five minutes passed, six, seven, and then Lord Hastings gave an expression of deep disgust.

"We have been discovered," he said. "Submerge five fathoms."

Jack gave the command and the periscope of the D-16 disappeared from view of that of the enemy.

"Sheer off to starboard," ordered Lord Hastings. "Should we maneuver aright, we may bring up with her."

The D-16 sheered off and dashed forward some distance ere Lord Hastings gave the command to rise that he might take another observation.

When the periscope was again above water. Lord Hastings looked quickly around, but could see nothing of the enemy; but even as he looked, the periscope of the enemy's vessel bobbed up less than half a mile away.

Quickly Lord Hastings gauged the range and shouted:

"Submerge! Quick!"

Down went the D-16, and at the same instant Lord Hastings ordered:

"No. 4 torpedo!" and giving the range as he had gauged it, commanded: "Ready!"

"Fire!"

For a moment after the "click" which told that the torpedo had been launched, there was silence. Then Lord Hastings signalled for a rise, that he might ascertain, if possible, whether the shot had gone home.

Greatly to his chagrin, he perceived the periscope of the enemy suddenly come up from below. Apparently it had submerged at almost the same instant as had the D-16, and had maneuvered out of harm's way.

"Missed her," he informed Jack.

At that moment the enemy's submarine dived, and Lord Hastings divined rightly that she was about to launch a torpedo at the D-16.

Quickly the course of the D-16 was changed, and she rolled violently as she suddenly turned her nose due south and sped forward.

Lord Hastings waited in some anxiety lest his maneuver had not been swift enough. Momentarily he expected to feel a shock that would tell him the Austrian torpedo had struck.

But no shock came and Lord Hastings breathed easier.

Then he bethought himself of some other plan and consulted Jack, the submarine, meanwhile, remaining far beneath the water.

"Other means having failed," said Jack, "I should say, use the searchlight and seek him out."

"I guess that is what will have to be done," Lord Hastings agreed.

He approached Frank's compartment, and himself took charge of the torpedo there, leaving Jack waiting at the periscope.

"We will run due west a quarter of a mile," said Lord Hastings to Frank, "and when I give the word flash your searchlight in all directions. The flash should blind the lookout on the enemy, and I will follow the sweep of your light with the torpedo. The moment I catch sight of the enemy I'll launch it, and we'll rise instantly."

Frank signified that he understood, and rapidly the submarine steamed ahead.

"Now!" cried Lord Hastings suddenly.

Frank released the powerful rays of the searchlight, and swept the sea to his right.

There was nothing to be seen.

Then he swept the sea to the left, and, less than a quarter of a mile away, the Austrian submarine was bearing down on them.

Lord Hastings, who had followed the searchlight with the torpedo, immediately launched it, and then, springing outside, gave the command to rise.

The D-16 leaped to the surface like a thing of life.

Lord Hastings took Jack's place at the periscope.

"Guess we got him that time," he said.

"Hope so," replied Jack briefly.

"I don't see," began Lord Hastings, "how — down quick!"

The submarine dropped like a log, and Jack exclaimed:

"What's the matter?"

"Missed her again," said Lord Hastings grimly.

"Why didn't you launch another when she bobbed up?"

"Because I was afraid she might do so first."

"Well," said Jack, "I have an idea that I believe will end this hide and seek business."

"Let's have it."

"Then let's go up. As soon as the enemy sight us, he will go down, expecting us to do likewise. But we'll fool him. We'll just shift our position a trifle — enough to be out of the way of a possible shot. Then we'll wait for him to come up again. In the meantime we'll train all our tubes along the water where he is likely to reappear. The moment he does so, you call the number within range and we'll get him."

"We'll try it," said Lord Hastings briefly.

Once more the signal was given to rise, and as the D-16 came to the surface, Lord Hastings, through the periscope, saw the periscope of the enemy go down.

Quickly the course of the D-16 was changed just enough to avoid a torpedo should one be fired by the enemy. Then Lord Hastings directed the training of the different torpedo tubes aboard the D-16.

All in readiness, they waited.

Suddenly Lord Hastings saw something emerging from the water. No. 2 torpedo was aimed directly at this point.

Lord Hastings wasted no time.

"No. 2!" he called.

"Click!"

There was no waiting for the command to fire. There was no time for it.

It had been Lord Hastings' intention to submerge immediately the torpedo had been launched, but so great was his confidence that this torpedo had gone home, that he allowed the submarine to remain on the surface.

"Did we hit her, sir?" cried Jack.

"She's gone," was the reply, "but I can't tell yet. If she comes up again we'll give her another."

Three minutes later and Lord Hastings gave vent to an exclamation of satisfaction.

"We got her," he cried.

Jack stepped to the periscope and peered through.

Less than a quarter of a mile away floated a mass of débris, all that was left of the Austrian submarine.

"You are sure that is part of her?" asked Jack.

"Positive," was the reply. "You can see part of her periscope among the wreckage."

Jack took another long look.

"You are right, sir."

"We may as well rise to the surface," said Lord Hastings, and Jack gave the command.

"Which way now, sir?" the lad asked.

"Back to the fleet to report," was the reply.

Jack descended below and gave the word.

Then he went to his own cabin, and drawing his pocket knife, set to work cutting another notch in the table.

Frank entered while his chum was engaged in this operation, but he did not interrupt until Jack had finished his task.

"Well?" he asked, as Jack leaned back with a sigh of satisfaction.

Jack looked up.

"Well what?" he demanded.

"How reads the score card?" asked Frank with a smile.

"Score card?"

"Yes, score card. What's the score; or, in the English of the British Isles, how many notches have you carved on that table?"

"Oh," said Jack, "I see. Why didn't you ask that in the first place?"

"Because," was the reply, "I am giving you a course in plain American. How many?"

"Seven," said Jack briefly.

CHAPTER XXIV.

OFF FOR THE DARDANELLES.

The chase of the Austrian submarine had been long and it was after nightfall when the D-16 again drew up in the shelter of the French fleet and Lord Hastings went aboard the flagship.

"Well, we got her," were Lord Hastings' first words to the French admiral.

"Good!" was the reply. "Tell me about it."

Lord Hastings did so, and the admiral was loud in his praises of the D-16 and her crew.

Then Lord Hastings bethought himself of the blowing up of the French cruiser.

"Were all members of the crew saved?" he asked.

"All but ten," was the reply. "They went down with the ship."

"Poor fellows," said Lord Hastings; "still it might have been worse."

"Yes, it might have been worse," replied the admiral, "and there might have been more sent to join them by the Austrian submarine had it not been for the gallant Lord Hastings and his crew."

Lord Hastings waved aside this praise.

"Come, come," he said, "we are too old in the service for such words. We do our duty as we see it, and that's all there is about it. Now if it comes to praise, I can remember the time when you — — "

"Enough!" cried the admiral, laughing. "As you say, we are too old in the service, you and I, for such words. Take the young fellows, now, and a word or two of praise, rightly spoken in the proper place, is an impetus to added bravery."

"And ultimate death for their foolishness," said Lord Hastings slowly.

"True; but what would you? Young blood, you know."

"Well," said Lord Hastings, "I must be going. I shall leave you in the morning."

"Headed which way?" asked the admiral.

"For the Dardanelles, to join the allied fleet."

"Mon Dieu! I envy you," said the old admiral. "Here I sit with nothing to do while you have all the fun."

"And what was it you said about young blood?" asked Lord Hastings with a laugh.

The admiral smiled.

"Oh, well," he said. "We sailors never grow old."

The two old friends shook hands affectionately, and Lord Hastings took his leave.

All was quiet on the submarine when he went on board, and he turned in at once. Not a man aboard the D-16 that night but slept a well-earned sleep, for the chase of the Austrian submarine, while not so long in itself, had, nevertheless, sapped the energy of all. The strain under which they worked — never knowing when a torpedo would send them all to their deaths — was tremendous.

All were up bright and early the following morning, however, and shortly after 7 o'clock the D-16 got under way. As she swung round and pointed her nose toward the Mediterranean there was a booming of guns from every ship of the French fleet and a cheer from the crews, for word of what the submarine had accomplished had spread rapidly, and officers and men alike joined in a parting ovation.

Through the Adriatic and into the Mediterranean went the British submarine D-16, speeding rapidly upon the surface of the water. Then she turned her head toward the east and Lord Hastings laid a course that, barring accidents, would quickly bring her to the entrance of the Dardanelles, where the allied fleet was still shelling the Turkish fortifications.

As they sped swiftly along, they talked of the war, of past adventures, of what lay in store for each in the future, and of many other things.

"And so Russia is to be given Constantinople," said Frank.

"Why not?" asked Jack.

"Why, no reason," replied Frank, "except that England has, heretofore, always opposed Russia's obtaining an outlet into the Mediterranean."

"War makes strange bedfellows," said Lord Hastings sententiously.

"It does," agreed Jack, "as is evidenced by the alliance of Germany and Turkey."

"How about England and Japan?" asked Frank.

"Oh," said Jack, "that's different."

"In what way?"

"Well, the Japanese are civilized. You can't say so much for the Turk. Besides, England's and Japan's interests in the far east are so closely allied that an alliance is not to be wondered at."

"Well, here is something I want to know," said Frank. "If Japan were to go to war with the United States, what would England do? Help her?"

"Why, no," said Jack. "Of course not."

"But the alliance?"

"In that event," said Lord Hastings slowly, "the alliance would be put aside. It is as though a man, who had formed an alliance with another, were asked to work against his own son or daughter. He wouldn't do it, and America is a child of England, after all."

"Well," said Frank, "I have heard many theories advanced. I just wanted to know yours."

No incident marred the peaceful progress of the D-16 as she made her way through the sunny waters of the Mediterranean. The weather was beautiful and Lord Hastings, Frank and Jack spent many pleasant hours upon the little bridge.

"How long before we shall reach the entrance to the Dardanelles?" asked Frank during one of these siestas.

"At the rate we are going," was the reply, "we should be there tomorrow morning. Of course, we might even do better than that, but I am in no particular hurry. There will not be much action before daylight."

"I suppose by this time," said Frank, "that progress in reducing the Turkish fortifications is swifter than before."

"It's hard to say," was the reply. "The outer forts are, of course, not so strong as the inner fortifications. As you know, having been there, the strait is very narrow, less than a mile in some places, and it is absolutely impossible for warships to force their way through without first destroying all guns on either side."

"But you remember our prisoner told us the Queen Elizabeth was wreaking great havoc with these. What do you know of her, sir?"

"Not as much as I should. She is the newest of Great Britain's dreadnoughts; and, without the shadow of a doubt, the most powerful sea-fighter afloat today. She carries the heaviest guns and outranges anything afloat. Shore batteries, powerful as they may be, are no match for her, for she can stand off at a distance of twenty miles and pound them with perfect safety to herself."

"She must indeed be a terrible engine of destruction," said Frank.

"She is," replied Lord Hastings calmly, "and eventually, mark me, she, and ships of her class, will be the means of bringing the Germans to terms, land victories of the most gigantic scale notwithstanding."

"Well, the sooner the better," said Frank.

"I agree with you," declared Jack.

"And I, too," remarked Lord Hastings.

It was just after daylight on the following morning that Frank, who was on the bridge, made out in the distance huge clouds of smoke and heard the faint sounds of booming guns.

"They are at it again," he told himself.

He went below and aroused Jack and Lord Hastings.

They were soon dressed and joined Frank on the bridge.

Every few seconds, above the sounds of the distant guns, one roared louder than the rest.

"The Queen Elizabeth," Lord Hastings explained. "Her voice is one that already must have carried terror to the heart of Constantinople and her people."

The speed of the submarine was increased, for Lord Hastings wished to arrive upon the scene as soon as possible. Gradually the forms of the huge ships of the allied fleet could be distinguished.

"Eighteen, nineteen, twenty," counted Frank. "I thought there were more than that. Where are the others?"

"Those you see now," said Lord Hastings, "have been left to guard the entrance to the strait. The others, the outer fortifications having been put out of commission, undoubtedly have progressed two or three miles into the strait."

"More than that, sir," said Jack. "You remember the prisoner told us they were reported to have progressed twelve miles."

"True, I had forgotten. I am willing to predict, then, that they have progressed farther by this time."

Lord Hastings' prediction proved correct; for when the D-16 drew up under the shelter of one of the largest of the battleships, and Lord Hastings went aboard, he learned that the Queen Elizabeth, leading the fleet, had progressed all of twenty miles and her great guns were now busily engaged in hurling huge projectiles miles farther.

From the commander of the British vessel which he boarded, Lord Hastings learned some of the details of the fighting up to date. He learned how, when it had been decided to attempt a passage of the Dardanelles, the Queen Elizabeth, fearless and powerful, had taken the lead, and had made short work of the outer defenses.

Her terrible projectiles had wreaked havoc upon the fortifications, and, when she had all but dismantled one, she moved on to another, leaving the smaller vessels to complete the work of destruction. And so on along the strait for twenty miles.

Word had just been received that the Turks were massing huge land forces, with heavy artillery, along the banks of the Dardanelles to attempt to check the onward movement of the allied fleet. Several of these forces had already been put to rout by the powerful and accurate fire of the warships, but now, it was said, a greater and more powerfully armed force was advancing to give battle.

Other than the success attained in the Dardanelles itself, the attempted passage had done two other things of benefit to the British cause. First it had forced the Turks to give up their proposed invasion of Egypt, and, second, it had caused the abandonment of the attempt to capture the Suez canal from the British troops, although it is doubtful if either would have terminated successfully for the Turks.

Lord Hastings returned aboard the D-16 and explained the situation to the lads.

"And what shall we do now, sir?" asked Jack.

"Well," said Lord Hastings slowly, "I see no use waiting outside and letting the other fellows do all the work. Guess we might as well go along after them."

"Good!" cried both lads in a single voice.

CHAPTER XXV.
IN THE DARDANELLES.

From the bridge of the D-16, Lord Hastings and the two lads viewed the terrible havoc wrought upon the Turkish fortifications by the guns of the allied fleet. Huge holes had been cut in the walls in some places, while at others the fortifications had been literally razed until there remained hardly one stone upon another.

Broken cannon were among the débris, shattered and in tiny pieces. Even now, after all this time, dead bodies, both of men and horses, lay here and there. All this the three upon the bridge of the submarine could see with their naked eyes as they made their way along the narrow strait.

"Terrible," said Frank.

"It is," replied Jack, "but it is also a stern necessity."

"Right," said Lord Hastings; "for once the Dardanelles is forced, and Constantinople is at our mercy, we have nothing further to fear from the Turks."

"And the Russians on the other side, in the Black Sea, what are they doing?" asked Frank.

"The best they can, you may be sure," replied Lord Hastings, "but not having the ships of our class they are at a disadvantage. Nevertheless, they will be in at the finish, I am sure."

"Then we shall nail them from two sides at once," said Frank.

"Exactly."

As the D-16 made her way up the narrow strait, the sounds of cannonading became louder, until, after half an hour's journey, it became a veritable roar.

"Great Scott!" shouted Frank. "This is awful. A fellow can hardly hear himself think."

Now the D-16 came within sight of the last of the allied vessels, and she was pouring her shells along the shore as fast as she could shoot. Other vessels ahead of her, now also in sight of the D-16 were doing likewise.

"Where is the Queen Elizabeth?" asked Jack.

"Oh, she is way up ahead," said Lord Hastings.

"Then that is the place we are bound for, I suppose," asked Frank.

"That is the place," replied Lord Hastings.

By one, two, ten, fifteen, nineteen ships the D-16 went, and then, just ahead, the form of the giantess of the sea loomed up. From her issued dense clouds of smoke, and her voice spoke in a terrible tone as she hurled her messages of death and destruction many miles farther than the eye could see.

This monster was the British Super-dreadnought Queen Elizabeth.

The two lads looked at her spell bound as she continued to spit fire and smoke, and in truth she looked like some monster of ancient fiction. In action as she was, she was indeed a wonderful sight.

"That," said Frank calmly, "is what I call a ship."

"Some ship, as you Americans would say," laughed Lord Hastings.

Right under the stern of the Queen Elizabeth, the D-16 came to a stop. The commander of the British dreadnought had noticed the arrival of the little vessel, and took the time to hail her. Upon learning that Lord Hastings was her commander, he invited him to come aboard at once.

"Would you like to go with me, boys?" asked the commander of the D-16.

"I should say we would, sir," replied Frank eagerly.

Jack also spoke in assent and five minutes later the three were aboard the Queen Elizabeth.

Lord Hastings presented the lads to the commander of the dreadnought, who spoke to them pleasantly. Then he and Lord Hastings retired for a few moments to the cabin, where they talked over the progress of the fighting.

"Well, boys," said Lord Hastings half an hour later, "we shall go back now, and when we get there I have a piece of news for you that will prove of interest."

Aboard the D-16 again. Lord Hastings did not give this piece of news at once, and finally Frank, becoming impatient, was moved to ask:

"And what is this piece of news that will interest us, sir?"

Lord Hastings smiled.

"Can't hold your horses a minute, can you?" he laughed. "Well, I'll tell you. The D-16 is going to take a little trip in advance of the fleet."

Frank's delight was so great that he hurled his cap into the air with a shout, and in coming down the wind carried it overboard.

Jack laughed.

"You see what too much enthusiasm gets you," he remarked.

"Never mind," said Frank after one regretful look at his departing headpiece, "I have another." He turned to Lord Hastings.

"What are we to do, sir?"

"Well, we are to try and establish the location of mines, draw maps of the fortifications, which may have been changed somewhat since the maps the admiral has were drawn, and learn anything else of value we can."

"I thought there would be fighting," said Frank, somewhat disappointed.

"Well, there is always liable to be fighting," said Lord Hastings. "In fact, any time you are around I am positive there will be fighting of some kind."

"And when do we start, sir?" asked Jack.

"As soon after nightfall as we are ready."

"But why wait for night?" asked Frank. "We are going under the water, aren't we?"

"Yes," replied his commander, "but we are likely to have to come to the surface at any time, and there is no need of taking unnecessary risks."

"That's true, too," said Frank. "But Great Scott! Night is a long ways off."

147

"In the meantime," said Lord Hastings, "I don't know of anything better than to watch the progress of the battle."

"We shall have to get closer than this if we expect to see anything," declared Lord Hastings.

He gave the command for fifteen knots, and gradually the D-16 forged ahead of the Queen Elizabeth and stood out before the whole fleet.

She made such a small speck as she floated gently upon the surface of the water, that Lord Hastings had no fear for her safety, and there she remained all during the day, while shells flew screaming past or cut up the water before and on all sides of her.

Twice the firing became so heavy that Lord Hastings deemed it advisable to submerge, and this was done. She reappeared in a new place each time, and her officers again ascended the bridge to watch the progress of the battle.

Along in the afternoon, the Queen Elizabeth, having almost dismantled two of the Turkish forts, steamed on past, unheeding the fire of their remaining guns and leaving them for her smaller sisters to dispose of.

Immediately their leader had made way for them, the other ships closed in and the fighting began anew, the new arrivals keeping the forts so busy that they had no time to pay further heed to the Queen Elizabeth, now farther up the strait, pouring her terrible shells into fortifications still farther along.

"At this rate," said Frank, "we shall be in Constantinople almost before we know it."

"Don't fool yourself," declared Jack. "Remember that in spite of the fact that the Queen Elizabeth is having apparently an easy time with these fellows, it will not all be smooth sailing. As Lord Hastings says, the further we progress the stronger the forts."

"I know; but she can stand off and batter them also."

"The trouble is that she cannot approach so close, and will have to depend more than ever upon the aviators to get her range; and it is more dangerous for the aviators over the inner forts."

"I suppose you are right," said Frank. "I hadn't thought of it in that way."

"How long do you suppose it would take us to get through the Dardanelles, sir?" asked Frank of Lord Hastings.

"Not long; why?"

"And coming out the other end we are in the Sea of Marmora, are we not?"

"Yes."

"And Constantinople is just across that?"

"Yes; but why these questions?"

"I was just thinking. It wouldn't be such a terrible job, in a submarine like ours, to run to Constantinople and sink a couple of ships. That would frighten the authorities so much that it might prove a benefit to the fleet here."

"True enough," said Lord Hastings. "But I don't believe we can afford to take such chances. If we should be sent to the bottom, we could never bring back the information we were after."

"Oh, I'm wrong again, as usual," said Frank.

"Don't think I am criticising," protested Lord Hastings. "The idea is first rate, and I feel certain we could get through in spite of the mines; but our first duty is to get the information we are sent out to obtain."

"That is true, of course, sir," agreed Frank.

Lord Hastings was lost in thought for some moments. Finally he said:

"I'll tell you what I will do. If we are successful tonight in getting what we go after, we will take a little jaunt on our own hook tomorrow night."

"Do you mean it, sir?" asked Frank eagerly.

"I do," said Lord Hastings.

"And we shall go to Constantinople?"

"If it is humanly possible to get there, yes."

Frank waved his hands in delight.

"Hurrah!" he cried. "We'll show these Turks a few things."

Even Jack was pleased, though he did not express his satisfaction in such a boisterous manner as did Frank.

"Yes, we shall show them a few things," he agreed.

"I wish this were tomorrow night," said Frank.

"There you go again," said Lord Hastings with a smile. "Just as impatient as ever. You will never gain anything that way, and, besides, it does no good."

"But I can't help it," protested Frank.

"You will have to get over it some day," said Lord Hastings severely. "You might as well start now."

"I'll try," Frank promised soberly.

Jack and Lord Hastings looked at each other and smiled.

"I'm going to hold you to that promise," Lord Hastings declared grimly.

CHAPTER XXVI.
SCOUTING.

"We may as well go up now."

It was Lord Hastings who spoke. For two hours, starting at nightfall, the D-16 had been creeping along under the waters in the Dardanelles. Submerging before she started, the submarine had not yet come to the surface once. But now, at Lord Hastings' words, Jack gave the command.

"Seems to me we should not be far from the opposite end," Lord Hastings continued.

Slowly the D-16 rose toward the surface, Frank, in the lookout room, meanwhile keeping a careful watch for obstacles ahead. There was little fear of encountering a hostile under-the-water craft, and for this reason the huge searchlight of the D-16 was allowed to play about the water, lighting it up for some distance on all sides.

The submarine reached the surface without trouble, and followed by Jack and Frank, Lord Hastings ascended to the bridge.

The water was very rough, and it was perfectly black outside.

"We could not have selected a better night," said Lord Hastings.

"But without a moon or light of some kind," asked Jack, "how are we going to make out the lay of the land?"

"We'll run inshore and do a little scouting," was the reply.

Accordingly the submarine was headed shoreward.

"The water here is deep enough to permit us to go almost to the bank," said Lord Hastings. "After that we shall have to swim."

When the D-16 had approached the bank as near as Lord Hastings deemed possible with safety, the commander turned the bridge over to Frank and announced that he and Jack would go ashore.

"But is there not fear of your being discovered?" asked Frank.

"We shall have to take that chance," was Lord Hastings' reply. "Now you stay right here with the submarine until daylight. If we have not returned, you will know that we have fallen into some difficulty, and you will return and report."

"Very well, sir," replied Frank.

Lord Hastings and Jack lowered themselves quietly into the cold water, and struck out boldly for the shore. They had to swim no more than a minute, when they felt the gradual rise of the land under their feet. Stepping softly, they continued their way, and soon stood upon dry land.

"Which way now, sir?" asked Jack.

"It doesn't make much difference," was the reply. "We'll go to the left."

They started out cautiously.

"Keep your eyes open," Lord Hastings instructed, "and your hand upon your guns. I don't fancy falling into the hands of the Turks."

"Nor I," replied Jack, as he followed his commander's advice.

The two stepped forward cautiously. They walked for perhaps five minutes, and then they brought up suddenly before a huge gray wall.

"Fort," said Lord Hastings briefly.

Jack said nothing, but followed his commander. Lord Hastings drew back a few yards and glanced up carefully.

"I'll get this in my mind," he whispered, "and draw my map later."

Jack nodded.

Lord Hastings scrutinized the fort carefully, and then with a nod, passed on. Jack followed.

For perhaps an hour they continued along the shore, Lord Hastings stopping now and then to take in some detail of the ground.

"We have reached the point where the Queen Elizabeth's shells have been dropping," he finally said. "There is no use going farther. Let us go back."

They turned and retraced their steps.

Arrived opposite the point where the submarine waited, they plunged into the water and swam back.

"We'll try the other side now," said Lord Hastings.

The submarine was guided close to the opposite bank, and once more the two plunged into the water and were soon ashore.

Again they proceeded for perhaps an hour, and again Lord Hastings discovered the effects of the Queen Elizabeth's shells. As he deemed it unnecessary to go further, they turned and once more retraced their steps.

They had almost reached the point off which the submarine waited when several figures loomed suddenly up in the darkness ahead of them. They were so close at this moment that it was impossible to avoid a collision. Jack, realizing this, and also knowing that the figures ahead must be enemies, did not wait for the latter to strike the first blow.

As he bumped into the man nearest him, he struck out heavily with his right. There was a fierce muttered Oriental imprecation and the man went to the ground.

Lord Hastings performed a similar operation upon the man nearest him, and he also toppled over. The rest drew back, and sent up a cry of rage. Realizing that their opponents would receive reinforcements in a minute, Lord Hastings and Jack sprang into the midst of them.

Striking out right and left, Jack disposed of two more of the enemy, and Lord Hastings a third; but at that moment Lord Hastings felt a sharp pain in his side and fell to the ground.

Warding off the blows of the one remaining assailant, Jack stooped over his commander.

"Hurt badly, sir?" he asked anxiously.

"Pretty badly, I fear," was the reply. "Caught me in the shoulder. Wait, I'll try to get up."

He made a valiant effort, but fell back with a moan of pain.

At the same instant the sound of running footsteps could be heard approaching.

Jack stooped over his commander and threw an arm about him.

With his feeble strength, the latter threw him off.

"Hurry!" he cried. "Save yourself! You can't get me away."

"You do as I say now," commanded Jack sternly.

He bent over.

"Put your arm around my neck."

Lord Hastings protested, but in vain. Jack raised his body and slipped an arm beneath it.

"Put your arm around my neck," he commanded again.

This time Lord Hastings obeyed. Jack lifted him up as though he had been a child, and turning, dashed for the spot off which he knew the submarine lay.

He had almost reached it, when he found himself suddenly confronted by two dark figures. Without a word he laid Lord Hastings gently upon the ground and hurled himself upon the men before him.

With two smashing blows—a left and a right—he laid two of them low before they could recover from their surprise, and as a third man, with a cry of rage, dashed upon him with upraised arm, Jack caught him by the wrist.

He gave a violent twist, there was a snap and a sharp cry of pain, and a knife fell to the ground. Jack planted his other fist squarely in the man's face, and even as the latter tumbled to the ground, the lad stooped over Lord Hastings and in another moment was running along the bank with him.

"You can't do it, Jack," gasped Lord Hastings, as the lad ran on.

"Keep still," ordered Jack. "I'll get you back aboard or break a leg."

Lord Hastings subsided.

Now Jack reached the point where the submarine lay only a few yards off shore.

"Drop into the water," he commanded Lord Hastings.

"But I can't swim with this arm," the latter protested.

"You do as I say," ordered Jack. "I'll get you before you go down."

Without further words, Lord Hastings obeyed, and as he disappeared from sight in the water Jack leaped lightly in after him. His hand touched his commander's collar before the latter had struck bottom, and coming to the surface, he supported Lord Hastings with one arm while with the other he struck out for the submarine.

Frank, upon the bridge peering intently into the night, had heard the sounds of confusion, but strain his eyes as he would, he did not make out the two forms in the water until Jack's voice, sounding almost in his ear, startled him.

"Lend a hand here, quick, Frank," came his friend's voice.

Quickly Frank leaped to obey.

Leaning over he held on to his commander while Jack scrambled aboard, and then both assisted their commander over the side, as gently as possible, so as to avoid straining his wound.

"Are you badly hurt, sir?" asked Frank, when Lord Hastings lay panting on the bridge.

"I don't know," came the faint reply. "But I have a nasty stab in the shoulder."

"We'll soon have that fixed up," said Jack cheerfully. "Help me carry him down, Frank."

With Lord Hastings stretched out in his bed, Jack ordered Frank to see about getting the submarine away from the dangerous location, while he tended to Lord Hastings' wounds.

"You'll have to hurry," he exclaimed. "They know we are around here some place, and they'll be after us like a pack of wolves."

Frank hurried back upon the bridge, to gain his bearings. As he emerged, a hand clutched him by the throat. In vain did the lad attempt to cry out. He struck blindly at his unseen opponent, who had grabbed him from behind.

Frank threw himself to the deck, and the man who had swam aboard the submarine fell on top of him. Taken at a disadvantage for a moment by Frank's ruse, his hold upon the lad's throat loosened.

At the same moment the submarine was made as bright as day by the powerful rays of a searchlight which fell upon it; but this glare was a boon to Frank, for it gave him a chance to determine his opponent's position, and he was not slow to take advantage of it.

With right and left he struck out swiftly time after time, and the Turk, badly battered, at last tumbled from the bridge and into the sea with a howl of pain.

At the same instant other figures began to clamber over the side of the submarine, where they had been attracted by the sounds of confusion.

Frank acted quickly. Jumping to his feet, he dashed below, closing the door to the bridge and conning tower after him.

"Submerge!" he cried as the doors came together with a clang.

In vain did the figures upon the top of the D-16 seek to retain a foothold. Their foundation slipped gradually away from them, until they were all left floundering in the sea.

Then the D-16 turned in the direction of the allied fleet.

CHAPTER XXVII.
A DESPERATE UNDERTAKING.

The D-16 made the return journey very slowly, for the master hand of Lord Hastings was lacking and Frank, being no navigator and his knowledge of the lay of the land very poor, was forced to proceed cautiously. In Lord Hastings' cabin, Jack was still busy dressing his commander's wound.

He found, after an examination, that it was not as serious as he had at first feared. The long bladed knife had caught Lord Hastings on the left side, halfway between the waist and the shoulder, and, turning up, had opened a deep gash clear to the shoulder. Lord Hastings was very weak, for the wound had bled profusely, but he was in no danger.

Jack performed a creditable operation upon the wound, and after he had bandaged it carefully, Lord Hastings lay back and went quietly to sleep. Then Jack took command of the vessel.

It was early morning when Jack gave the signal to rise, for he wanted to be sure that he had passed all danger points before coming to the surface. When they did bob up from beneath the water, he found that he had gone too far by more than a mile. However, no harm was done, and the D-16 was quickly brought about and soon lay under the lee of the Queen Elizabeth.

Here she lay till midday when Jack went aboard to report. The commander was very anxious when he learned that Lord Hastings was wounded, but he accepted Jack's report instead and announced that he would visit Lord Hastings some time during the day.

"Well," said Frank to his commander as he sat at his side, "I guess this settles our Constantinople trip."

"Why so?" asked Lord Hastings.

Frank was surprised.

"Why we can't go with you in this condition," he replied.

Lord Hastings smiled faintly.

"A little thing like this is not going to stop me," he said. "True, I can do no fighting, but I can still navigate the boat."

"But it is impossible," said Frank.

"No, it is not impossible," said Lord Hastings. "We shall go."

At this moment Jack came in, and when he learned what Lord Hastings proposed to do, he attempted to dissuade him. So did the commander of the Queen Elizabeth when he came to visit Lord Hastings that afternoon.

But the commander of the D-16 was not to be dissuaded.

"I am the commander of this vessel," he said grimly, "and when I give an order I want it obeyed. Mr. Templeton, you will get under way an hour after nightfall."

Jack saluted. He said nothing, for he knew that to say anything would be useless. He had never seen his commander in just this frame of mind before, but he was smart enough to realize that Lord Hastings meant what he said.

Night fell. An hour later, in accordance with his orders, Jack gave the signal, and the D-16 sank slowly from sight.

Lord Hastings called Frank.

"Help me to my place at the periscope," he said quietly.

"But, sir," protested Frank.

"There are no buts," said Lord Hastings. "Help me to my post."

Frank said nothing further, but obeyed.

Seated in a chair beside the periscope, Lord Hastings took a long breath. Then he called to Jack.

"I'll do the watching here," he said. "You run the ship in response to my signals."

Jack saluted.

Frank took the lookout, as usual, and once more the huge searchlight lighted up the water under the Dardanelles.

The time wore on, still all stood at their posts. Morning came and Lord Hastings said:

"According to my calculations we should now be in the Sea of Marmora. We will go up for a look about, Mr. Templeton."

The D-16 rose until her periscope showed Lord Hastings the signs about her.

"Very good," he said slowly. "You may go down to your previous depth."

The D-16 sank again.

"See anything, sir?" asked Frank.

"Enough to know that my calculations were correct and that we are in the Sea of Marmora."

"Any vessels in sight, sir?"

"Couple of merchantmen, as nearly as I could make out."

"Did they see us, sir?"

"I think not. In fact I am sure of it."

"That's good, sir."

"So it is. You may proceed at twenty-five knots."

The D-16 gathered headway and soon was traveling along under the water at a great rate.

"Won't we have to be careful of mines along here, sir?" asked Jack.

"I do not believe they have mined much as yet. They figure that there is little danger of the Allies forcing an entrance for some time to come. However, we may as well be careful. Take the lookout, Mr. Chadwick."

Frank saluted and returned to his post.

"The only place we shall have to be really careful," said Lord Hastings, "is when we near Constantinople. No matter how safe the Turks may have felt, it is hardly possible they have not taken all emergency precautions."

"If not," said Jack, "the German officers who have been put in charge of their forces will have done it for them."

"I guess there is no doubt about that," was the reply. "The Germans are thorough in everything they do."

"Shall we land in Constantinople, sir?"

"I think not—unless it is necessary for some purpose that may arise later. Right now I see no need of landing."

"There are sure to be Turkish warships there, sir?"

"I should think so, surely."

"When do you reckon we shall reach there?"

"I had planned to enter the harbor about midnight."

"Best time for such work, sir."

"We'll be aided by a moon tonight—or should be, at least."

And it was midnight when the D-16, with her deck barely awash, drew into the harbor of Constantinople, slinking silently along, with every man at his post, seeking out her prey.

"Warship dead ahead," called Lord Hastings, and gave the command to stop. "We couldn't want a better place to launch a torpedo," he added. "A miss at this distance is out of the question."

The crew stood at attention, and action came swift and fast.

"Fire!" came the command at last.

A torpedo sped on its way.

Immediately the D-16 darted away to a safe place, and then arose to the surface to see the result of its work.

A half moon lighted up the scene about them, and Frank and Jack ascended to the bridge. Lord Hastings remained below.

Of a sudden a terrible din broke the stillness of the night. Hideous cries went up into the sky. Searchlights broke forth and swept the harbor. Aboard the Turkish warship, the victim of the submarine's torpedo, confusion reigned. Officers tried in vain to restore some semblance of order among the crew until they could ascertain the extent of the damage done.

It was impossible. Never the coolest sailors in the world, the Turks lost whatever courage they may have possessed and a panic ensued aboard the wounded warship, which soon spread to other vessels in the harbor. There seemed to be no doubt in the mind of any as to the cause of the explosion.

"We'll go down and try another one," said Jack calmly.

They descended below, and a few moments later the D-16 was moving toward another victim. This ship and then a third were torpedoed with unerring aim, and the panic which followed above was terrible to behold.

In the city itself word of the disaster spread, and the Sultan and his cabinet, believing that the fall of the capital was imminent, hurriedly got together what papers of state they could lay their hands upon, and dashed in automobiles from the city.

"Well," said Jack to Lord Hastings, "I guess we might as well call it a good night's work and let it go at that."

"I am of the same opinion," replied his commander. "We must have created a terrible furore."

"There is not much question about that," said Frank with satisfaction. "I would like to go ashore and see what is going on."

"I wouldn't object to that either," said Jack.

"It's impossible," declared Lord Hastings. "You would surely be captured."

"I don't think so," said Jack. "In this confusion a boat could easily be launched and no one would be the wiser. Then, if you remained right here, we could return without trouble."

"Besides," interposed Frank, "we might be able to learn something of advantage."

"What do you say, sir?" asked Jack.

Lord Hastings hesitated.

"I should say no, of course," he replied at last, "but I find it hard to deny you boys anything. I suppose it could be done, if you exercised the proper precautions."

"We will, sir," broke in Frank. "Have no fear of that."

"Nevertheless, it is just that that I am fearful of," said Lord Hastings slowly. "You see, I know you of old."

"Then we can't go, sir?" asked Frank, greatly disappointed.

"I didn't say that," replied Lord Hastings.

"Then you mean we can, sir?"

"Well, yes, if you will give me your solemn promises to be very careful."

"We will do that, sir, won't we, Jack?"

"We will," was his friend's reply.

"In that event," said Lord Hastings, "you have my permission to go. You will also promise to return within three hours."

"We promise that also, sir," said Jack.

"Then you may go; but if I were you I would remove your uniforms and don civilian clothes. Then you may pass muster anywhere, as there are many foreigners in the city."

Jack and Frank heeded this advice, and hastened to their cabin to change their clothes.

CHAPTER XXVIII.

A CAPTURE.

In the little boat, in dark civilian clothes, the lads put off from the submarine, and soon were mingling with the hundreds of other little craft darting shoreward as fast as strong arms could drive them.

"I guess we shall make it all right," Frank whispered to Jack.

"Of course we shall," was the reply. "It'll probably be harder getting back."

"We'll come through some way," was the reply.

"Of course."

At that moment Frank's attention was directed to a struggling knot in the water.

"What's that?" he asked drawing his friend's attention.

"Looks like a fight to me," said the latter.

"Let's go closer and have a look."

The lads steered the boat closer to the struggling heap, where they were able to make out three men fighting desperately, while nearby was an overturned boat.

"One of them looks like a white man," said Jack.

"In that case we shall have to give him a lift," said Frank.

"Remember what Lord Hastings said," Jack warned his chum.

"But we can't stand idly by while a couple of Turks drown a white man."

"No, we can't do that," Jack agreed.

With long powerful strokes they sent their boat closer. Then Jack was able to distinguish the faces of the combatants.

"Two Turks and a German officer," he said. "I can't see why we should interfere on his behalf."

"He is white," protested Frank.

"Right," said Jack. "That puts a different face on the matter, of course."

The boat was right up to the struggling trio.

"No use wasting our energy," said Frank.

He stood up in the boat and brought his oar down upon the head of one of the Turks. The latter disappeared beneath the water without a sound. Frank turned upon the second one, but he had seen the fate of his comrade and had no mind to share it. He released his hold upon the German officer and made off.

"Let the German swim to his boat. We don't want to be bothered with him," said Frank.

"Suits me," said Jack.

Frank sat down, and the lads would have rowed off; but at that moment the German disappeared beneath the water.

"Tired out, I guess," said Jack. "Well, we can't stand by and see a man we have just rescued drown without raising a hand. I'll have him in a minute."

He dived overboard, and reappeared an instant later holding the German by the arm.

"Help me get him in," he said.

Frank obeyed, and Jack climbed in after him. The German lay in the bottom of the boat, exhausted.

"Talk German when he comes to," Jack warned. "There is no use letting him suspect anything."

"All right," said Frank, and while Jack sent the boat shoreward with long and powerful strokes, he attempted to revive the man they had saved.

The shore was but a short distance away when the German showed signs of returning consciousness. He moaned feebly and turned on his side. Frank slapped his hands and rubbed them vigorously, and soon the German attempted to rise.

Frank lent him a helping hand, and the German at last managed to sit up with Frank's shoulder as a support. Then his eyes roved about and he took in the situation around him.

"And so you saved me," he said to Frank.

"Well, my friend and I together," replied Frank, also in excellent German.

"Those scoundrels would have killed me," said the German officer.

"So we noticed," replied Frank. "What was the matter?"

"Well, I was swimming in the water, and they refused to take me aboard. You see, in spite of the fact that we are doing our best for this benighted country, we Germans are not loved here."

"I know that," Frank agreed.

"When they refused to assist me into their boat, I became angry and tried to pull myself aboard. They hacked at my hands with knives, and the best I could do was to accidentally pull the boat over, throwing them into the water. Then they attacked me."

"And no wonder, at that," said Frank drily.

"Well, that's true. Still they should have let me in their boat."

"I am not disputing that," said Frank. "Where do you wish us to put you ashore?"

"Wherever you chance to land."

Frank nodded.

"But who are you?" continued the German.

"Just a couple of noncombatants," replied Frank briefly.

"But you are German?"

"Well, yes, partly so. Also we are Americans."

"Caught here at the outbreak of the war?"

"Yes."

"Well, I'll do what I can to get you out of it."

"Thanks."

"You see, I am not without influence. It happens that I am the new military governor of the city."

"Is that so?" exclaimed Frank in surprise.

"Yes. I only arrived today, and was having a consultation with the Turkish admiral when this disaster occurred."

"Have you any idea what caused this disaster?" asked Frank quietly.

"I guess there is no doubt what caused it. A British or a French submarine."

At this moment Jack took a hand in the conversation.

"You say you are the new military governor of the city?"

"Yes."

"Then you know something of the plans of defense?"

"Well, rather. I have them in my pocket."

"Then," said Jack, "I should say that you are a very indiscreet sort of a military governor."

"What do you mean by that?" asked the German, half rising.

Jack's reply was addressed to Frank.

"Cover him with your gun, quick!" he commanded. "Don't let him get away."

Although taken by surprise, Frank acted quickly. His gun leaped from his pocket and was levelled at the new German military governor of Constantinople.

"What's the meaning of this?" demanded the latter angrily.

"The meaning is that you are our prisoner," replied Jack quietly. "Turn her about, Frank," he added, "and we'll go back to the submarine."

"Submarine!" exclaimed the German. "Oh, I see, you are British."

"You bet we are," replied Frank.

The German grew silent, and Jack, who was watching him carefully even as he rowed, noticed that he was fumbling in his breast pocket.

"Watch him, Frank," he cried. "Don't let him throw anything overboard."

Frank leaned forward and pressed the muzzle of his automatic against the German's breast.

"No tricks," he said quietly, "or you are a dead man."

The German's hand dropped to his side.

The lads rowed back to the submarine quickly. Frank jumped aboard first and Jack waited until the German had followed him before he climbed up and drew the little boat up after him. Then all went below, Frank keeping his weapon on the German as they descended.

Lord Hastings came bustling out.

"Back so — —" he began, and stopped in surprise at the sight of the third man. "What is this?" he demanded.

"This," said Jack, with a flourish of his hand, "is the new German military governor of Constantinople."

"But," said Lord Hastings, "why do you bring him here? What do we want with him?"

"He told me, confidentially," said Jack, "that he carries the Turkish plan of campaign."

Lord Hastings understood in a moment.

"In that case," he said, "we want him badly. Mr. Military Governor, you are indeed welcome."

"And the first thing to do," said Jack, "is to get the papers before he can get rid of them."

"His Excellency will give them to us, I am sure," said Lord Hastings.

"I will not," growled the German.

"Then we shall have to take them," said Jack.

He stepped suddenly forward and seized the German in a firm embrace.

"You take them while I hold him," he called.

In vain did the German struggle. Jack held him firmly while Frank and Lord Hastings explored his pockets and took therefrom every piece of paper they could find. Lord Hastings glanced them over carefully.

"They are all here," he said. "You can let him go now."

Jack stepped back and the German shook himself angrily.

"You'll pay for this," he shouted angrily.

"Why, we expect to," said Lord Hastings smoothly, "we expect to pay for it with our big guns, which, with the help you have extended to us by giving us these plans, will make the task easier."

The German doubled his fists and took a step forward.

Jack smiled at him.

"I wouldn't even think of it if I were you," he said quietly.

The German drew back.

"And shall we let him go now?" asked Lord Hastings. "He is simply a burden to us, you know."

The German's face lighted up.

"We can hardly do that, much as we would like to," said Jack. "You see, he might tell them all ashore that we have their plans, and they would naturally change them. As it is, believing that he has been drowned, the Kaiser will simply appoint a new military governor and use the plan of campaign already decided upon."

"True," said Lord Hastings. "Then we must keep this capture a secret."

"Yes, sir," said Jack, "and now we may as well get away from here."

"In the meantime," replied Lord Hastings, "his excellency shall be our guest. You may give the word to submerge, preparatory to departure, Mr. Templeton."

Jack turned away.

CHAPTER XXIX.
THE LAST SHOT OF THE D-16.

Running smoothly and swiftly the submarine passed from the Sea of Marmora back into the Dardanelles, and set out on the last lap of her journey. It was now after 7 o'clock in the morning, and a grey mist, heralding the approach of a storm, was in the air above.

Gradually the swell of the waves increased as the wind grew in violence, and the waters of the strait grew angry. But below, where the D-16 moved swiftly along, all was smooth and tranquil, although the barometer showed a heavy disturbance above.

The new military governor of Constantinople, desiring the freedom of the vessel rather than to be confined, had given his parole, and, seeming to take his plight with fortitude, was watching the workings of the vessel with the greatest interest. Some of the intricate details Lord Hastings took the trouble to explain to him.

Then, just as the D-16 seemed about to accomplish the last lap of her return journey safely, the trouble occurred.

Lord Hastings had given it as his opinion that they must at that moment be in the very heart of the Turkish fortifications in the strait, and had turned away, when the prisoner, with a sudden leap, sprang to the signal that controlled the air tanks. Before any one could stop him he had given the signal that sent the D-16 soaring to the top of the water, where she floated upon the surface not a hundred yards from the guns of the nearest Turkish fort.

The wind had kicked the strait into an angry swirling mass of water, with the waves running high. But the D-16 had hardly been tossed upon the crest of the first wave when a Turkish sentry espied her.

He gave a hoarse cry, and in another moment a big gun spoke.

"Boom!"

The D-16 staggered. One more huge wave she climbed, and when she settled into the trough of the sea with it, she went deeper.

She seemed to turn on her beam ends as she dived, but suddenly she righted herself. Officers and crew picked themselves up from the positions into which they had been flung, and rushed for their posts.

"Look at the tanks!" cried Lord Hastings, and Jack rushed to obey.

He came running back an instant later.

"A miracle," he cried. "The tanks are full. That is what brought us down."

Lord Hastings stared at him in surprise.

"Impossible," he said. "How could the tanks be full?"

"I don't know, sir," replied Jack, "but they are."

Lord Hastings thought hard and fast.

"Where did the shell strike us?" he asked at length.

"Just forward of the tanks, sir."

"That may have had something to do with it," mused the commander, "although I can't see how. Give the command to rise two fathoms, Mr. Templeton."

Jack obeyed. Once, twice, thrice he gave it, with no result. Then the man who had answered the signal came running into the cabin.

"Something wrong, sir," he said quietly. "I can't budge her, sir."

"You mean you cannot force out the water?" asked Lord Hastings quietly.

"Yes, sir."

"It is as I feared," said the commander. He turned to officers and crew who had gathered about. "It is all over," he said quietly. "We are done for. If we cannot force the water from the tanks, we cannot go to the surface. It is impossible to fix the break beneath the water. That is all, men."

As the men started slowly from his cabin, Lord Hastings raised a hand.

"One moment," he said quietly. "There is a chance for all but one of us. As I am the commander of this vessel, and should be the last to leave, that one shall be me."

"What do you mean, sir?" asked one of the men, stepping forward.

"The torpedo tubes," said Lord Hastings quietly. "All but one of us can be shot to the surface by means of the torpedo tubes."

The face of every member of the crew lighted up with hope.

"Are we still moving ahead?" asked Lord Hastings.

"Yes, sir," replied Jack.

"Good, at what speed?"

"Fifteen knots, sir."

"All right. In another three quarters of an hour we will be beneath our own fleet. There we shall stop. Then, one at a time, you men will climb into the torpedo tubes and I will launch you safely. This has been done more than once, and in spite of some slight pain and inconvenience, there is no danger."

"But you, sir?" asked Frank. "How will you get out, if you remain to send us?"

"Why," said Lord Hastings quietly, "being the last man, I shall not get out."

Jack jumped to his feet.

"I'll not hear of it!" he exclaimed. "If you stay, I stay."

"And I, too!" declared Frank, taking his place by his friend's side.

Lord Hastings opened his lips to protest, but Jack took the words out of his mouth.

"It's no use, sir, we mean it," he said firmly.

A sailor approached and took his stand alongside the two lads.

"Neither will I go," he said quietly.

A second sailor fell in line, the engineer, another sailor, the chief gunner's mate, until finally the entire crew of the D-16 had expressed their determination to die with their commander.

Now the German prisoner spoke.

"It is useless for us all to die," he said quietly. "Why not draw lots and see who shall stay? That is fair to all. I myself shall draw with you."

Each member of the crew looked at the other. Slowly all nodded their heads.

"I protest," said Lord Hastings. "I am the commander of this ship, and shall be obeyed."

"This is one time, sir," said one of the sailors, "when we shall refuse to obey your orders. Let us draw lots."

"One moment, men, before we draw," said Jack. "I just want to say that Frank here and myself have been close chums. If I should happen to have to stay, I want his word, and that of Lord Hastings, that neither will insist on staying with me."

Frank looked at Lord Hastings, and the latter looked back at Frank.

"I agree," said Lord Hastings finally, "with the proviso that the same rule applies should I have to stay."

"And I agree under the same conditions," said Frank.

"Good!" said Jack briskly. "Now as to the method. How shall we draw?"

An old sailor stepped forward.

"If you please, sir," he said, "I have an old pack of cards in my pocket."

"Very well," said Jack, "a pack of cards will serve as well as anything else. Just how shall we decide?"

The sailor spoke again.

"There are twenty-six of us here," he said, "because I have counted us all up. In the pack of cards are fifty-two — two to a man. Let the ace of spades be the death card. Whoever draws the ace of spades stays."

"So be it," said Lord Hastings. "Give me the deck, Grigsby."

Grigsby produced a dirty and grimy pack of playing cards, and gave it to Lord Hastings. Slowly the commander of the D-16 counted the cards to make sure they were all there, then shuffled them gently. Next he placed the deck in the center of the table in the middle of the room and turned to Frank.

"Cut," he directed briefly.

Frank advanced to the table with steady tread, and with as steady a hand cut the cards.

"Now," said Lord Hastings, "let us all stand around the table, and, each in turn, draw a card. The man who draws the ace of spades stays. Is it understood?"

There was a general nod of assent, and all gathered around the table. Lord Hastings stood first, next was Jack, then Frank, then the German prisoner and following him the sailors.

"I shall draw the first card," said Lord Hastings, "and then the draw shall pass around to my left. Here goes!"

Midst a death-like silence he stretched forth a hand and drew a card, which he exposed to the view of all. It was the ace of clubs.

Jack stretched forth a steady hand, and drew the two of spades. Frank drew the five of clubs, and the German the ace of diamonds.

The draw came again to Lord Hastings and the ace of spades was still hidden in the deck.

The silence was even more pronounced as Lord Hastings drew his second card and slowly held it up so that all might see.

It was the king of spades.

"Pretty close," he said quietly.

"But not close enough," said Jack with a laugh. "I believe I can do better myself."

Quickly he stretched forth a steady hand and drew a card, which he threw down upon the table, face up.

A gasp went round the circle of faces.

The card was the ace of spades.

Jack turned to Lord Hastings with a faint smile.

"You see," he said steadily. "I was sure I could beat you."

When Jack drew the fatal card, Frank stared at it as though dumbfounded, and for a moment was unable to speak. Then he rushed upon his friend, and threw his arms about him.

"But I won't let you stay alone," he cried.

Jack pushed him gently away.

"Remember our agreement," he said quietly.

Lord Hastings approached and laid his hand on Frank's shoulder.

"Jack is right," he said. "An agreement between gentlemen is not to be set aside for any reason. Be sure that I feel just as deeply as you, but I am older and not so much given to showing my feelings."

He walked over to Jack, and held out a hand.

"I am sorry it was not me," he said quietly.

"And still," said Jack, taking the hand, "it won't be so awfully bad, will it, to be the one who fires the last shot of the British Submarine D-16?"

"We should now be directly beneath the British fleet," said Lord Hastings, after a glance at his watch.

"Good," said Jack. "Then we may as well stop the engines."

This was the work of an instant.

"How deep are we?" asked Jack.

"Quarter of a mile," replied Lord Hastings briefly.

"Then the pressure will not be so bad for you fellows," said Jack.

He stepped to No. 1 torpedo tube and examined it.

"All right," he said. "The only trouble you may have is that you will not be seen when you reach the surface. However, that is the chance you will have to take. Just keep your senses, and when you reach the surface swim until you are picked up. How does the barometer read?"

"Clearing," replied Frank, after a quick glance.

"Good! I was afraid it might be stormy above."

He paused and looked around. All was in readiness.

"Now," he said, "the longer you stay here the more danger. The sooner we get it over with the better. You first, Lord Hastings."

"No," replied Lord Hastings. "I shall be the last to go."

Jack bowed.

"Very well," he said. He turned to Frank. "Come, Frank," he said. "You first."

"Not me," Frank protested. "I'll wait until the rest have gone."

"Have your own way," said Jack. He turned to the German prisoner. "You first, then, sir," he said calmly.

The German bowed.

"It might as well be me as another," he said.

He stepped to the torpedo tube and crawled in.

"Lucky I am not too big," he said cheerfully.

"Ready?" asked Jack.

"Ready," came the reply.

"Click!"

Just this faint metallic sound and the human torpedo sped on its upward journey like a catapult.

Jack turned to Grigsby.

"You next," he said.

Grigsby crawled into the tube.

"Ready?" asked Jack.

"Ready, sir," came the reply.

Again the click and the second human torpedo sped on its way to safety.

And so on down the line, until there remained, besides Jack, only Frank, his chum, and Lord Hastings, his commander.

Jack turned to Frank.

"It's your turn, Frank," he said.

Frank hung back.

"Let Lord Hastings go first," he protested.

Lord Hastings raised a hand.

"I am still your commander," he said severely. "You will crawl into the tube, sir."

Frank looked long at him, and again started to protest. Lord Hastings' face was inflexible.

Frank drew himself up to attention.

"Very well, sir," he said quietly.

He approached Jack and held out his hand, which the latter grasped with vise-like fingers and squeezed.

"Goodbye, Frank," he said softly. "Remember that I am glad to do this for you. I have no one in the world, while you still have a father and friends at home. Take my advice and return to your own country. Our war is none of your quarrel."

Tears came into Frank's eyes as he gripped his chum's hand. A lump came into his throat.

"Goodbye, Jack," he said with an effort.

He staggered toward the tube, and Lord Hastings helped him in. "Get it over quickly," he exclaimed.

"Ready?" asked Jack.

"Ready," replied Frank in a choking voice.

"Click!"

Frank went hurtling on his way to safety.

Jack turned to Lord Hastings.

"I am glad you stayed until last," he said very quietly. "I feared that Frank would make a scene. Thank you."

"I did it for your sake," was the low response.

"Well, now it is your turn," said Jack. "Come, sir. Let's have it over with."

"Cannot I prevail upon you to let me take your place?" asked Lord Hastings earnestly. "You are so young, while I, well I am old, and it will make no difference."

"You have Lady Hastings to think of," replied Jack, "and I have no one at all."

"But— —" began Lord Hastings.

"Come, sir," said Jack, "don't shake my resolution now. I lost. It is up to me to pay. Remember our agreement."

"True," said Lord Hastings.

He held out his hand and Jack grasped it.

"I wish to say," said Lord Hastings, "that it has never been my pleasure to know a braver and more courageous lad. I am proud to know you."

"And I," said Jack, "am proud of having had the chance to serve under you, sir."

They gripped hands tenderly for the space of a few seconds; then, without another word, Lord Hastings relaxed his pressure and stepped to the tube. Jack assisted him, and then called out:

"Ready?"

"Ready," came the reply. "Goodbye, Jack."

The last words were lost in the click of the torpedo and Jack was left alone.

He walked to his own cabin and sat down upon his bed. Then, rising, he approached the table and ran his fingers over its edge, counting the notches.

"Fifteen," he said to himself. "Well, that's not so bad. Now, I wonder how long I shall have to wait."

He drew his revolver from his pocket and looked at it long and earnestly.

"No," he said aloud, and thrust it back into his pocket.

Then he sat down to await the moment when the D-16 must split open as the result of the death blow she had received.

When Jack released the catch that sent Frank flying into space, the lad's breath was taken away by the force of his upward flight; but a moment later he felt himself upon the surface of the sea and cooling draughts filled his lungs. Sputtering and gasping he inhaled great breaths, and then, mindful of Jack's injunction, he set about keeping himself afloat.

Rescue was near at hand; for the first of the sailors had already been picked up by the crew of a British warship, and had told his story. Small boats now floated about looking for other arrivals from the deep.

A boat approached Frank and he was dragged over the side. Then he lost consciousness. He was taken aboard the warship and put to bed immediately, as was Lord Hastings when he was picked up a few moments later.

To Jack, sitting below in the doomed submarine, came thoughts of the past. In his mind he reviewed his meeting with Frank, and later, with Lord Hastings. Memories of the earlier days of the war came back to him vividly and he recounted to himself the dangers he and Frank had faced together.

"Oh, well," he said at last, "it is all over now."

He arose and made his way toward Lord Hastings' cabin; but even as he set foot over the threshold, the D-16 gave a sudden lurch.

"Guess this will finish it," said Jack aloud.

But, to his amazement, the submarine, instead of going deeper, seemed to be rising. With a faint hope fluttering in his heart, Jack glanced at the indicator.

It was true. The D-16 was going up—not down.

Jack stared at the indicator like one fascinated.

"Six fathoms, five fathoms, four fathoms," it read.

Jack was moved to action.

"There is still a chance," he told himself. "I know the submarine is wounded unto death, but if she should happen to leap clear of the water, I must be prepared."

He ascended the steps toward the bridge, and stood close to the door that would give him life should the D-16 really come to the surface, if only for a moment.

With his hand upon the lock, Jack waited, his eyes, meanwhile, still fastened upon the indicator, which he could barely see from his present position.

"Two fathoms," it read, "one fathom, half a fathom," and then Jack suddenly threw open the door, and with a single jump, was upon the bridge, even as the D-16 leaped clear of the water for a brief instant, before she settled again, to rise no more.

That brief instant was enough, for in it Jack was able to hurl himself clear of the vessel, into the sea, where he struck with a loud splash, and a shock at the icy coldness of the water.

The lad did not even lose consciousness, but struck out vigorously for what he saw was a British warship.

A sailor espied him, and a boat put off after him. Five minutes later he was lifted aboard, where he promptly succumbed because of the reaction.

He was put to bed alongside Frank and Lord Hastings.

Frank was the first to open his eyes. He glanced about him. There, to his left, lay Lord Hastings still unconscious.

In a flash it all came back to Frank and he buried his face in his arms.

"Poor old Jack," he said. "I wish I could have stayed in his place."

At that moment a figure on the other side of him moved. Faintly interested in spite of his grief, Frank turned to see who it might be. As his eyes fell upon the figure, which was now rising to a sitting posture, they almost bulged from his head, and he cried out in a voice of amazement:

"Jack!"

Jack looked around slowly.

At first he was unable to gain his bearings, but in a moment the past came back to him.

He reached out and took Frank by the hand.

"Yes, it is I," he said quietly. "I had a most miraculous escape. I'll tell you about it."

"Don't tell me now," said Frank, squeezing his chum's hand. "It's enough for me to know that you are alive."

An officer entered.

"I thought you would be glad to know," he said, "that we are about to get under way for home."

"I'm glad," said Frank simply.

Lord Hastings' joy, when he recovered consciousness and learned that Jack had not perished beneath the water, was unbounded, and during the long journey back to England they often talked of his miraculous escape.

And so, while they are enjoying the rest they deserve, as they are being carried back to the shores of old England, we will take our leave of them — Frank Chadwick, an American youth with all the courage of his forebears, Jack Templeton, than whom no braver youth ever breathed, and Lord Hastings, British nobleman — their commander and friend.